The Druid's Gift

The
Druid's Gift

Margaret J. Anderson

Alfred A. Knopf

New York

For Norman

This is a Borzoi Book published by Alfred A. Knopf, Inc.

Copyright © 1989 by Margaret J. Anderson
Jacket illustration copyright © 1989 by Nigel Chamberlain
Map copyright © 1989 by Anita Karl and James Kemp
All rights reserved under International and Pan-American Copyright
Conventions. Published in the United States by Alfred A. Knopf, Inc.,
New York, and simultaneously in Canada by Random House of Canada
Limited, Toronto. Distributed by Random House, Inc., New York.
Manufactured in the United States of America
Book design by Elizabeth Hardie

2 4 6 8 0 9 7 5 3 1

Library of Congress Cataloging-in-Publication Data
Anderson, Margaret Jean. The druid's gift / by Margaret J. Anderson.
p.   cm.
Summary: Given the gift of seeing the future, a young girl, living on
the tiny and remote island of Hirta at the time of the druids, is able to
travel forward in time and experience some of the important events that
shape the history of her island home.
ISBN 0-394-81936-5 ISBN 0-394-91936-X (lib. bdg.)
1. Saint Kilda (Scotland)—History—Juvenile fiction.
[1. Saint Kilda (Scotland)—History—Fiction.
2. Druids and druidism—Fiction.   3. Space and time—Fiction.
4. Islands—Fiction.]   I. Title.
PZ7.A54397Dr   1989   [Fic]—dc19   88-22028

TABLE OF CONTENTS

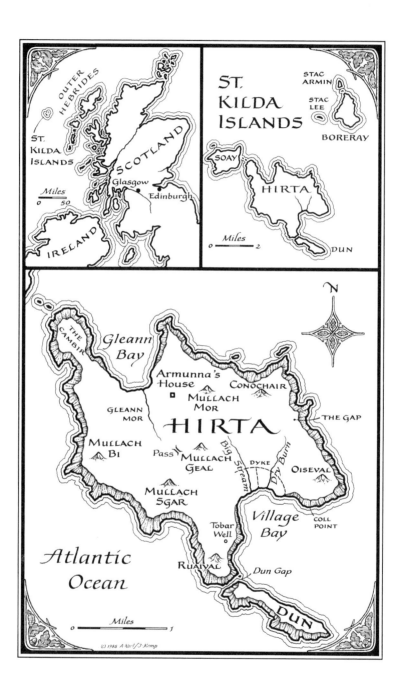

OUTER HEBRIDES

ST. KILDA ISLANDS

SCOTLAND

Glasgow

Edinburgh

Miles
0   50

IRELAND

ST. KILDA ISLANDS

STAC ARMIN

STAC LEE

BORERAY

SOAY

HIRTA

Miles
0   2

DUN

N

THE CAMBIR

Gleann Bay

Armunna's House

CONOCHAIR

MULLACH MOR

GLEANN MOR

HIRTA

THE GAP

MULLACH BI

Pass

MULLACH GEAL

Big Stream

DYKE

Dry Burn

OISEVAL

MULLACH SGAR

Village Bay

COLL POINT

Atlantic Ocean

Tobar Well

RUAIVAL

Dun Gap

DUN

Miles
0   1

© 1988 A. Karl / J. Kemp

AUTHOR'S NOTE

The St. Kilda Islands—Hirta, Soay, Boreray, and Dun—lie 112 miles due west of the Scottish mainland. They were first described by Donald Monro, who visited them in 1549, though his book wasn't published until 1774, which must be something of a record in the publishing world!

I learned about St. Kilda years ago when a zoology professor told us that on those remote, treeless islands wrens had evolved into a separate subspecies from their woodland-dwelling relatives in Britain. Then eight years ago I came across an article about people who had lived there for generation after generation on a diet of seabirds—fulmars and puffins—that they harvested on the steep cliffs. Centuries earlier, as a result of good luck or genius, someone had developed a Stone Age food drier called a cleit. The St. Kildans were thus able to dry bird meat for the winter in spite of the wet climate. Cleits were also useful for storing rawhide ropes, sheepskin cloaks, and peat for the fire. I was fascinated to find that people as well as birds had adapted to those lonely islands, and I was sure there was a story in it. I began to read everything I could find about the islands. Finally the story emerged as *The Druid's Gift*, part fantasy because St. Kilda is fantastic, and part history and legend.

Toward the end of the nineteenth century, steamship travel brought St. Kilda closer to Britain and the British closer to St. Kilda. This was the age of the Victorian naturalist. The St. Kilda wren was threatened with extinction by eager egg collectors. An Act of Parliament in 1904 saved the wren, and there are now over a hundred nesting pairs on Hirta. The people weren't so fortunate. Contact with the outside world lured away many of the young men. The people who were left became dependent on goods from Britain, but they had nothing to trade in exchange. Fulmar oil and feathers weren't in big demand on the mainland. By 1930 only thirty-six people were left, ten of them belonging to one family. They petitioned the British government to resettle them on the Scottish mainland.

The islands now belong to the National Trust for Scotland and are managed as a nature reserve. In July 1988, I took part in an archaeological dig on Hirta. As our boat approached the island over a glassy sea and the stark cliffs of Hirta emerged from the thick mist, fantasy gradually taking the shape of reality, I felt nervous. It was like meeting someone face to face that

I'd fallen in love with from a few snapshots and letters!
We rounded the headland of Oiseval and anchored in
the bay. I hadn't imagined the hills would be so green
and inviting. The old pictures I'd pored over were in
sepia tones or black and white.

The archaeological dig was fascinating. While scraping down through field drains from the fifteenth or
sixteenth century, we uncovered the complete skele-
ton of a dog. A dog that had been tossed into the ditch
after it died—around four hundred years ago. I felt as
if I were one of my own characters going through a
time slip! We discovered quite a lot of early pottery, so
coarse and rough that it was hard to tell it from stone.
The most important find didn't look like much at
all—a piece of shaped soapstone deep in the soil. The
nearest place soapstone occurs naturally is Norway, so
that fragment of stone was a link with the Vikings.

But the real story of Hirta wasn't buried beneath the
soil. The memory of the St. Kildans lingered everywhere: in the empty cottages along the village street, in
the stone cleits that crouched on the hillsides like
ancient tortoises, and in the old graveyard where
yellow irises were growing among the simple stone
markers. When we climbed to the Gap and watched
the fulmars riding the winds against the cliffs of
Conochair or when we followed the sheep tracks up
the thrift-covered slopes of the Cambir, we walked in
St. Kildan footprints.

Ten years after Alexander Ferguson left the island

he wrote, "I think there is no paradise on earth like it." I can second that. Though, of course, I haven't seen St. Kilda in the dark months. And I didn't have to swing down the cliffs after birds—I only tried to capture them on film. And never once were we served boiled fulmar or dried puffin meat for dinner!

The Druid's Gift

I
The Samain Feast

A SLANTING RAY of sunlight pierced the clouds, turning the waves in Village Bay from sullen gray to silver. A good omen, but no one saw it. The islanders were huddled indoors waiting for evening, for this was Samain, the day when all the spirits of the afterworld were loose on the island. At sunset the Stallir, chief of the druids, would call the wandering spirits back to the Place of the Dead—though not until the islanders had presented him with a share of the bird harvest. Those who didn't give generously ran the risk of being pursued by lingering spirits during the dark months; those who didn't keep enough for themselves would be stalked by hunger before the birds came back.

Inside one of the small dark houses that dotted the hill above the bay, Tormod Rudh had just finished filling a large basket with meat.

"Do you think that's enough, Morag?" he asked his

young wife as he sat down beside her to share the warmth of the glowing peat fire.

"Aye, it should be," Morag answered. "And we have plenty of food left in the storage cleit to see us through the winter."

"We don't want to risk angering the druids—or the spirits—by offering too small a gift," Tormod said worriedly. "Especially not now."

Morag smiled, feeling her child stir in her womb. She reached out for her husband's hand and placed it on her belly so that he could share her joy.

"It's a lad, for sure!" Tormod said, his face creasing with happiness, as it always did when he spoke of the coming child. "And he's going to be strong and quick. A lad to share my rope when I hunt gannets and fulmar on the cliffs. With him to look after us, we'll never go hungry, even when I grow too old to climb down the face of Conochair."

Morag tossed some bracken onto the glowing peat. A bright tongue of flame licked up the dry leaves and then died away, leaving the hut darker than it had been before.

"Maybe we could spare a few birds for Fearg Dubh to take," she said quietly, staring at the fire, not wanting to see the surprise in Tormod's face.

But the surprise was in his voice.

"Fearg Dubh! He would never be able to pay us back! He'll not go down the cliffs after birds again.

Besides, the Stallir would know the offering wasn't from Fearg, so what good would it do?"

Two summers ago a fall on the cliffs had left Fearg Dubh with a stiff leg and twisted shoulders. His face was twisted, too—as much from the cold inner anger of not being able to climb as from the throbbing of his injuries. Last summer Morag had seen him digging puffin eggs from the burrows near the cliff because he no longer had the quickness to catch grown birds with a fowling rod. He wouldn't be able to scrape together much food for the druids. But Tormod was right. They'd know the meat didn't come from Fearg. With the spirits of the afterworld on their side, the druids knew everything.

"If there could just be more understanding between us and them." Morag sighed. "On so small an island, scarce half a day across at a child's pace, the people should not be divided."

"Our only hope for peace lies in driving the druids out," Tormod answered. "The Old One can remember back to the time before they came here, and she says people didn't go hungry then."

"And in those days there was no more to life than catching birds and plucking them! When the druids came, they brought with them their wisdom and music and the memory of another world. Don't forget that they foretell the wind and the weather. They know the feast days and can name the stars. If we could just learn a little of their music and magic . . ."

"And would you know the dark side, too?" Tormod asked, getting to his feet. It was almost time to go. Morag remained silent.

The dark side: the part of druid magic that they never put into words, as if the mere mention of it could make it happen.

Pulling their long sheepskin cloaks close about them, Morag and Tormod Rudh stepped outside into the wind-driven rain. Most of the other islanders were already on their way up the hillside to the Place of the Dead, some with bundles on their backs, others carrying baskets between them. They were a small-boned people, with wild black hair and cheeks reddened by the constant wind and rain, though from a distance they looked more like a straggling line of sheep. The children dashed ahead like playful lambs, scuffling in the withered bracken and chasing one another through the heath. After spending all day cooped up indoors, neither their parents' uneasiness nor the wild weather could dampen their excitement at being outside again. By the time Morag and Tormod Rudh caught up with the rest, they had reached the Place of the Dead and even the children had fallen silent, their faces taking on a solemn look. They stood around the huge wet mound of driftwood and heather and bracken that had been gathered for the fire, their dark eyes fixed on the top of the pass leading over to Gleann Bay.

"Here they come at last!" Morag breathed.

A whisper ran through the crowd. The little ones nervously burrowed against their parents' legs as the column of white-clad druids flowed down the hillside toward the Place of the Dead. They walked three abreast, the outer flanks headed by the seer and the bard, the middle column led by the Stallir, who carried the sacred flame from Gleann Mor. The magic fire that burned without fuel. The flame that neither rain nor wind could extinguish. When the druids reached the Place of the Dead, they split into two groups, the seer and the bard leading them into a half circle, leaving the Stallir in the center of the arc, facing the islanders.

Morag's eyes shifted from the tall figure of the chief druid to Feadair, the young bard, who was standing near her. His hood had slipped back, and his long hair, which she remembered from the last feast day as red in the firelight, now looked dull brown in the rain. The Stallir was speaking in a high, keening voice, asking the spirits to protect the old and nourish the weak through the dark months. It crossed Morag's mind that some would likely join the spirits before the sun returned no matter what the Stallir said or how much the islanders gave, and she edged closer to Tormod Rudh. She comforted herself with the thought that spirits of the afterworld would never claim a child who kicked so strong, although three months must still pass before it would be born.

Then the Stallir called on them to present their gifts. The islanders bent down to pick up their baskets and creels and began to shuffle forward. The Old One went first, her leathery, wrinkled face scarcely visible under the hood of her cloak. Morag's heart ached when she saw Fearg Dubh's offering—a few eggs in a basket lined with dulse. His twisted face was wet with rain; spit dribbled from the corner of his crooked mouth, glistening on his black beard. The Stallir's eyes were hard and cold as he watched Fearg Dubh place his basket on the growing pile. But now it was Morag's turn. She and Tormod carried the heavy creel between them and then hurried back to where they had been standing.

After all the offerings had been presented, the Stallir looked toward Conochair. Standing motionless as a gannet frozen in flight, the folds of his white robe draped from his upraised arms, he called the spirits back to the Place of the Dead. Three times he called them. Three times Morag thought she heard a sound in the wind like the rush of beating wings.

Then the chief druid turned back to the islanders. "Some of the spirits are angered by the meagerness of your offerings," he shouted. "I cannot be sure that all of them answered me."

"If we were to give you more, we wouldn't have

enough meat left to keep ourselves fed until the birds come back!" the Old One answered, her voice shrill with the memory of other years when hunger had driven them to do things best forgotten. The old woman wasn't afraid to challenge the Stallir. Her gift had been generous. She was well paid for attending births and brewing remedies for sicknesses, and this winter her storage cleit was full.

"The oat field was flattened by rain and the storms kept us from going over to Boreray after gannet eggs," Gareth complained, but he spoke without the Old One's conviction, as if the demands of the druids, like changes in the weather, were beyond his control.

The Stallir heard them out and then lifted his torch and thrust it into the heart of the pile of wood. As the flame caught hold, hissing along a branch despite the lashing rain, the mood of the islanders shifted. Soon the rich smell of roasting mutton would fill the air.

Running his fingers over the strings of his harp, Feadair, the bard, began to play. Morag recognized Feadair's music at once. It was the tune he'd played in the spring at the Beltane fire, and it was often in her mind. Their eyes met, and Morag knew that he, too, remembered the night of the Beltane fire. Reaching into the pouch she carried under her cloak, her fingers traced the outline of the token the bard had given her that night. Rough, like a withered oak leaf, and hard and cold, yet not made of stone. When Feadair added his voice to the music, Morag was glad that the sheepskin cloak hid her swelling belly. She dropped her gaze and pressed closer against Tormod Rudh.

While the men rounded up the fattest sheep to roast over the fire, the women carried the druids' share of the harvest to the storage cleits in Gleann Mor on the north side of the island, where the druids lived. Morag's back ached from the weight of her load and she had trouble keeping her footing on the mud-slick path, but all the same she was glad to miss the killing of the sheep. It wasn't really the killing she minded. It was more the way it was done. The Stallir with his gleaming knife . . . the animals' terror . . . and the blood-smeared stone . . .

By the time Morag returned to the fire, the druids had gone back to Gleann Mor. She smiled at the children wrestling and tumbling in the heather, their black hair slicked down by the rain, and tried to imagine her own little one among them in a few years. Tormod Rudh saw her and fetched a hunk of meat from the spit. After tearing it in two with his teeth, he handed her a piece dripping with fat.

"That's too much!" she protested, but she took it anyway.

While she was eating, she caught sight of Fearg Dubh standing alone in the shadows beyond the circle of the firelight. She went over to talk to him, but by the time she reached the place where she'd seen him, he had disappeared. Perhaps he hadn't really been there. Perhaps it had been his likeness conjured up by the Spirit Host.

Morag shivered and was suddenly afraid, knowing that Fearg would not be with them when the birds came back in the spring. But her fear wasn't just for Fearg Dubh. It was also for herself.

2
CAITLIN

SHRIEKING WINDS BATTERED the island and drove the waves against the rocks with such force that spray showered down on the village as salt rain. Inside the earthen house on the lower slopes of Oiseval, Morag was unaware of the raging storm. She knew nothing beyond the pain and the struggle of bringing her child into the world. Even the Old One's herbal brew brought no relief.

"It will soon be over," the Old One promised.

Tormod Rudh, sitting against the far wall, beyond the flickering light of the fulmar oil lamp, didn't dare ask the meaning of the Old One's words. He tried to keep his mind on the rope he was plaiting. A man's— or a lad's—very life depended on the strength of his rawhide rope. But the next moment a thin sound, like the mewling of a hungry sea swallow, brought him to his feet. He stumbled across the room.

"It's a girl child," the Old One said quietly, laying the babe at her mother's breast.

"A girl!" Tormod repeated stupidly.

Then he saw that Morag, her eyes misted with pain, was trying to speak. He leaned over her to catch the words.

"We'll name her Cat . . . Caitie . . . Caitlin," she whispered weakly.

"We can think on it," he answered.

Morag moaned and her whole body shuddered in protest.

"Caitlin it will be, then," Tormod agreed quickly. "Though I don't know where you came up with such a name!"

"You must take care of her, Tormod! Say that you'll care for her."

"Aye, I'll do that," Tormod promised, but he wasn't sure that Morag heard him. Her eyes were closed and her breath was coming in short bursts. Then she began to cry out again, and the Old One pushed him away.

"Go fetch your sister Rona!" she said, snatching up a bundle of sphagnum moss to staunch the bleeding.

Hearing the dreadful urgency in the old woman's voice, Tormod Rudh made for the door, without wasting time on questions. Once outside, he was surprised to find that it was light. The wind was dying, but the waves still thundered up the beach and the sky was ragged with clouds, layered like the gray and white of a ruffled fleece on a sheep's back. Tormod set off down the hill.

He was almost at the Big Stream when a flicker of movement high above the towering bulk of Mullach Sgar caught his eye. A flight of birds streaming out of the west. For a glad moment, he thought that the birds had come back early to ease the islanders' hunger, but then he saw that they were flying in the shape of the crescent moon. The Sluagh! The Spirit Host had come to claim his beloved Morag! He turned and ran back up the heather-clad slopes of Oiseval and burst into the house.

The old woman was leaning over Morag's still figure, murmuring softly, and Tormod allowed himself to hope. But then she turned to face him and he saw the tears coursing down her withered cheeks.

"Her spirit's left her, Tormod . . ."

"Morag . . . Morag!" Tormod sobbed, throwing himself down beside his wife. "I would have gone in your place."

The Old One tried to find words of comfort, but it was the baby's insistent crying that finally broke through the shell of Tormod's grief. She was lying on the earthen floor close to the fire, swaddled in a lambskin blanket. When Tormod Rudh bent to pick her up, the Old One made a quick move as if to stop him, but the child grew quiet at the feel of her father's arms around her. She nuzzled her face against his chest. Tormod carried her to the doorway so that he could see her better. He drew a sharp breath of dismay as he pulled back the blanket. The baby's head was covered with hair as golden as the celandine that grew by the Big Stream in the springtime. But all the island children had thick black hair! Then the bairn turned her head and looked up at Tormod Rudh, dark-eyed and wrinkle-browed, and it was as if his own face was staring up from the clear water of the Tobar Well. The ridge of the brow, the dark eyes, sharp cheekbones, and wide mouth.

"Caitlin," he whispered, smiling at the sight of his old face on this child so new, and a gaze so wise and knowing besides.

"Caitlin," the Old One repeated. "I never heard the name before."

Later in the day, when Rona saw the fair-haired babe lying in the makeshift cradle beside the fire, she wouldn't go near her.

"She's no child of yours," Rona told Tormod Rudh. "Look at that hair! She's a changeling left by the faerie folk. Give her back to them, Tormod, or she'll bring you nothing but grief."

"Give her back?" Tormod repeated.

"Aye! Leave her by the Tobar Well on Ruaival. She'll be gone by morning. The faeries always take back their own when they see they're not wanted."

"I promised Morag I would care for her," Tormod said quietly. "I had hoped you would foster her."

"I'll not nurse a fair-haired changeling alongside my little Morda!" Rona answered.

"She's Morag's bairn!" Tormod shouted angrily. "But we don't need your help. The Old One will care for the child. After all, she gave Morag a home when her mother died."

"That dried-up old woman!" Rona said. "How is she going to feed a baby? The ewes have no milk, and it's too soon to find eggs. The few scraps of meat left on the floor of the storage cleit are tough, even for those of us who have teeth."

"I'll search the hills until I find a ewe that has lambed early," Tormod answered. "I'll bring the sheep back and pen her in Village Bay so that the Old One and I can milk her."

"I never thought I'd see the day when Tormod Rudh chose to do women's work!"

The baby whimpered and Tormod Rudh gently gathered her into his arms, his ridged brows meeting in a frown. His expression exactly matched that of the infant scowling in his arms.

3
A Shared Rope

ALTHOUGH CAITLIN THRIVED, she wasn't an easy child
to raise. She never seemed to need much sleep, and she
was already running about at an age when other babies
still crawled. She talked early, too, and was full of
questions. Her light hair made people uneasy, as did
Tormod Rudh's devotion to his child. The islanders
wouldn't let their own children play with her. Even
the Old One sometimes muttered that Caitlin was a
changeling after all, yet she flew into a rage if anyone
else hinted at it.

As the years passed, Caitlin's hair grew darker and
became deep reddish gold, as if it had been touched by
the afterglow of the setting sun. By the time she
reached her seventh summer, the islanders had all
grown used to her and their children wanted to play
with her, but Caitlin preferred climbing the rocks with
Tormod Rudh. She wanted to go everywhere with
him. When he wouldn't take her along, she amused

herself by scaling the big boulder below the house. The Old One grew hoarse from shouting at the child to come back down.

One summer morning, when the tide was low, Tormod Rudh went in search of gulls' eggs. He had crossed the wrack-slick rocks that separated Dun from Hirta and was halfway up the steepest crag when he heard a scuffle below him. Looking down, he saw little Caitlin working her way steadily up the face of the rock.

"Go back, lass!" he yelled. "You can't come up here. The footholds are too far apart."

"I can do it," the child insisted, her hands spread like starfish as she stretched her fingers to reach a crack in the rock above her head.

"Go down, Caitlin!"

"I can't!"

Tormod couldn't tell if Caitlin spoke out of stubbornness or fear, but with her directly below, he could only continue upward. He pulled himself onto the top of the cliff, then turned around and peered back over the edge. Caitlin was now a long way up, her red-gold head drawing steadily closer. When she stopped, Tormod held his breath, willing her not to lose her grip. He watched anxiously as she explored the rock face with her toes and finally found a narrow ledge. As soon as she was within reach he grabbed her and dragged her up over the lip of the rock in a rattle of falling stones.

"I wanted to do it all by myself!" Caitlin said, scrambling to her feet. She stood on the very edge of the cliff, disdainful of the emptiness behind her, scowling up at him. Tormod's fright dissolved and he grinned down at his small, fierce daughter. She smiled back. They both knew she had just proved she was as nimble and fearless as any lad.

After that, it was a common sight to see the two of them hunting eggs and catching birds on the crags of Dun or on the rocks of Ruaival. But there was one place that Caitlin was not allowed to go. When Tormod climbed the cliffs of Conochair, he went only with the men. The sloping shoulder of Conochair rose smoothly up from Village Bay, but the mountain had no back to it, dropping sudden as death, a sheer wall against the sea a thousand feet below. Birds beyond counting nested on the ledges and crevices of the cliffs, and each summer the men of the island swung down among the birds on rawhide ropes as fearlessly as if they too had wings, harvesting meat and eggs to fill their storage cleits against the dark months.

"Why can I not go down Conochair?" Caitlin asked her father one evening when he was getting his rope ready for the next day's climbing.

"Because you are a girl," the Old One said, speaking from the dark recess of the sleeping crub.

If Caitlin had seen the Old One in the bed, she certainly would not have chosen that moment to mention climbing on Conochair.

"I can climb as well as anyone," she argued. "I'm as tall as my cousin Dougal, though he's four years older, and I can run as fast as any boy."

"The spirits would not look kindly on a lass on Conochair," the Old One replied. "Hunting is for the men."

Caitlin scowled. The old woman was forever nagging Tormod Rudh, saying that Caitlin should be doing girls' work—tending the oat field and milking the ewes and plucking birds—and not running wild, searching out gulls' eggs and snaring guillemots.

"You babble like the water of the Big Stream," Tormod always answered.

But like running water, the Old One's nagging began to wear Tormod down. He urged Caitlin to spend more time with the other girls close to her age—Una and Beitris and her cousin Morda.

And then in the summer of Caitlin's fourteenth year, Tormod Rudh put an end to all Caitlin's dreaming by asking Rona's youngest boy Dougal to share his rope. With four older brothers, there were lads to spare in that family. Caitlin could have borne the hurt better had it been anyone but Dougal. He was a dour, quiet lad, with no laughter in him. And though he wasn't spiteful like his mother Rona, Caitlin always felt disapproval in his eyes when he looked her way. Her own eyes were gray and stormy as the winter sea as she watched her father and Dougal stride off together for the cliffs of Conochair on the first morning of the fulmar harvest. Tormod Rudh had his rawhide rope looped over his shoulder, while Dougal carried the long-poled fowling snares.

"My father should have taken me," Caitlin raged. "He shouldn't be risking his life with that yellow-faced sheep. Dougal's hands'll be slimy with sweat and his knees aquiver just looking over the edge of Conochair."

"Hold your tongue, lass," the Old One answered briskly. " 'Tis only a fool who does not know fear on the cliffs. There's work enough to do here, or run off and help the girls pluck the birds."

Caitlin couldn't bear to stay inside the hut with the Old One, so she went to look for Morda and Una and Beitris. If it hadn't been for that old woman's nagging, she thought, Tormod Rudh would surely have chosen her instead of Dougal to share his rope.

The girls were working on the shady side of the village dyke. They made room for Caitlin to join them without breaking the rhythm of their plucking and chattering. Flying feathers tickled their noses and made them sneeze, and by midafternoon their woolen shifts were stained with oil and fat. Although the girls' fingers were as quick as their tongues, the pile of pale, limp carcasses didn't seem to grow any larger, nor the pile of unplucked birds any smaller. Only the feathers seemed to multiply. Suddenly Caitlin jumped to her feet, too impatient and restless to pull another feather.

"I'm going over to the stream," she said, tossing a

half-plucked fulmar back onto the pile. "Is anyone else coming?"

"But . . . but the birds . . ." Una stammered.

"They can wait," Caitlin answered, although she knew this wasn't true. There was never enough time to pluck and split and gut and dry all the birds before the weather broke.

"Maybe we could go just long enough to cool off," Morda suggested, looking uncertainly at Caitlin and then at Una and Beitris.

Dougal's sister was the last person Caitlin wanted for company today, so when Una pointed out that ravens or wandering dogs might get the birds, Caitlin dashed off without waiting for the argument to be settled. She went bounding through the cool, springy grass of the meadow, her long hair streaming behind her. When she reached the Big Stream, she knelt down and splashed her face and arms with the cold water, trying to rid herself of the smell of fulmar oil. Then she waded upstream, listening to the music of the islands—the sighing wind, the pounding waves, and the crying birds. After leaving the streambed, she continued to climb, heading for the top of the pass. From there she could look down on Gleann Mor and see the sacred oak trees—the only trees on the whole island. They grew close together, blasted and bent and twisted and yet hardened by the salt-laden winds. Beyond the trees Caitlin could make out the stone walls that curved like a ram's horns around the forecourt of Armunna's House, the huge underground dwelling place of the druids. Within those walls burned the magic fire. Caitlin's heart beat a little faster when she saw several white-hooded figures emerge from the doorway. They headed toward the oak grove.

She was glad that she was alone. All the others were afraid of the druids and often whispered together about the dark side of the druid magic. They were as bad as the Old One, making up stories to frighten themselves.

The harpist's music, echoing the sad song of the winds along the cliffs and the cries of the birds against the clouds, drifted up from the oak grove. As Caitlin listened, the music seemed to weave a spell around her. Hidden by bracken fronds, she started to work her way down the hillside on her hands and knees, pushing between the rough brown stems. The bracken eventually gave way to woody heather, but she crept still closer.

Feadair, the bard, was sitting under a tree, with the sacred antlers of Oiseval bound to his head and his long hair red against the whiteness of his cloak. He was singing about a time long ago when their four islands—Hirta, Soay, Boreray, and Dun—had all been joined and the land had stretched like the water all the way to the far horizon. Caitlin listened, entranced. In those days there had been no need to use a boat to reach the faint blue land that shimmered in the east on a clear day. In those days, too, the people on

Hirta had been giants, and Armunna had been the greatest of them all. She used to run with her hounds to the place where the sun and the sky met, and she had captured the great deer on the highest peak of the Hebrides. She ate its flesh and brought its horns back to the sacred heights of Oiseval. There were no deer on Hirta now, and Caitlin doubted that there could be animals anywhere in the world with horns that twisted like the branches of an oak tree.

Even after the druids went back to Armunna's House, Caitlin stayed where she was. Feadair's story seemed to fill the empty places in her mind with pictures. She stared up at the blue sky, trying to recall the exact rhythm of the bard's words. The brittle heather gave little protection from the sun, and she drowsed a little, letting Feadair's song become part of her own dream. But then the dream took a new turn, a dark, frightening twist like a hovering shadow. She opened her eyes to escape from it—and there stood the Stallir towering over her, his hood thrown back to reveal hair the color of sun-bleached thatch. The eyes staring down into hers were winter blue. No word was spoken, only a long, hard look given. Then he was gone.

Caitlin lay limp in the heather, feeling as if she had been branded by the Stallir's eyes, the way Brus the shepherd marked the lambs. When her strength came back, she scrambled to her feet and raced up the hillside, ducking from rock to rock as if she were being chased. Caitlin reached the top of the pass, then skittered down the Big Stream, scraping her knees against the boulders. She didn't stop at the dyke, where the girls were still patiently plucking birds, but ran all the way to her own house on Oiseval, arriving there breathless and still trembling.

When Caitlin threw herself down in the grass, the Old One hardly looked up. She was sitting in the doorway, up to her elbows in blood and muck, beheading and gutting a pile of plucked birds. Her old friend Druag sat near her, hunched forward to catch what she was saying. He could not hear well now and was no longer agile enough to swing down the cliff after fulmar, though he could still anchor a rope and thus earn himself a small share of the catch.

"The good weather'll break before the meat is dried," Druag was saying. "When I was up at the Gap this morning, I saw clouds gathering over the island of Boreray."

"Aye, and so the storage cleits will not be filled," the Old One said. "Yet the druids will expect as much as we gave them last year."

Caitlin reached for a splitting stone and picked up a bird. Perhaps she could forget the Stallir's strange eyes in the busyness of the harvest—though with the Old One and Druag talking about the druids it wasn't likely. She spread a cleaned bird on the drying rack and grabbed another.

"If the harvest is poor, maybe people will listen to Gareth when he says the time has come when we should drive the druids out," Druag said.

"How can we do that when they control the spirits of the afterworld?" Caitlin asked impatiently.

"I'm not saying there is no risk," Druag answered. "Though by themselves the druids are no match for us in courage. Even the Stallir wouldn't dare go down Conochair in the spring, with the birds beating the air with their wings to protect their nests."

Caitlin shrugged. She knew nothing would come of Druag's bold talk. The younger men, like her own father, wouldn't listen. They could give to the druids at Samain and feed their families as well. Only those with nothing to lose could afford to risk their lives for the sake of change—men too old to climb, like Gareth and Druag, or fatherless bairns, or women with no husbands to provide for them.

"If only there were more understanding between us and the druids. . . ." Caitlin sighed.

"There are times when you put me in mind of Morag, lass," the Old One said.

"I never knew my mother had hair the color of the oak tree in autumn," Caitlin answered. "And was she tall?"

"It wasn't her looks I was thinking of. It was more the restlessness in her—and the way she didn't have the same thoughts as everyone else. Many's the argument I had with her over the druids! She used to say that we should all become one people and I would tell her that she might as well say that puffins and fulmars should lay eggs in the same nest."

"Morag had her own reasons for believing that!" Druag said, giving Caitlin a long, knowing stare that made her feel faintly uneasy.

"Fetch us some more birds, Druag," the Old One snapped. "With Caitlin here to help me, we'll soon have these cleaned, and you yourself were saying that the weather may change."

Druag pushed against his cane as he struggled to his feet.

"Tell me about my mother and about the night that I was born," Caitlin said, watching the old man walk slowly down the hill. She had heard the tale before, but today she wanted to hear it again.

"It seems but yesterday!" the Old One said softly. Her eyes had taken on a distant look, but her hands were still tearing the innards from the birds. "You came into the world at the dark time of the year, your newborn cry a thin echo of the screaming wind outside. Indeed, it was such a wild night that seven sheep were blown clear off Conochair. Toward dawn I sent your father, Tormod Rudh, to fetch his sister Rona to be with you, because I couldn't leave poor Morag's side. But on the way he saw the Sluagh—birds flying together in a crescent moon—and he knew that it had come to take your mother. By the time he got back here, Morag's spirit was gone."

"And he gathered me up in his arms and carried me to the door, that he might see me better," Caitlin prompted.

"Aye," the Old One agreed. "I had wanted to hide you away from him, for I knew he was disappointed that you were not a lad, but he took to you in spite of you being a girl and having light-colored hair."

Caitlin frowned at the mention of Tormod Rudh having wanted a lad. It reminded her that he was out on Conochair sharing his rope with Dougal. So Dougal was to take the place of the lad he'd never had.

"And Morag? Did she want a son?" Caitlin forced herself to ask.

"Morag wanted a lass. Even when she was carrying you, she knew you'd be a lass. And on the night you were born she told your father you were to be named Caitlin. I often wonder about that, for it is not a name of our islands."

"I'm glad my mother named me," Caitlin said. " 'Tis the only thing of hers I have."

"She did give you something else," the Old One said slowly, scrabbling in the pouch she carried at her waist. "On the night you were born Morag entrusted me with this token. She said that I would know when it should be yours. I think that time has come—even though it speaks of things I do not understand."

The token she held out to Caitlin shone like the

evening sun reflected in the water of the Tobar Well. It was crumpled like a withered oak leaf, and when Caitlin took it, she found that it was hard and cold. She stared at it for a long time.

It didn't seem to bring her mother Morag any closer.

4
THE SPIRIT HOST

THE FULMAR HARVEST was almost at an end. The islanders were weary of plucking and gutting and carrying. Weary of oil and feathers. And Caitlin was weary of the other girls' chattering and bickering. Swinging a creel of dried fulmar onto her back, she set off for the farthest storage cleit on the side of Ruaival. Being alone would make up for the effort of carrying the heavy load so far.

She had almost reached the cleit when a shadow darkened the ground ahead of her. Glancing up, she saw that it wasn't a cloud passing between her and the sun, but a flight of birds. Birds streaming over the crest of Mullach Bi. As she watched they drew closer together and seemed to become one, taking on the crescent shape of the new moon. The creel slipped from her shoulders, spilling some of the dried meat onto the ground, but she was only aware of the birds.

The Sluagh—the Spirit Host—foretold a death!

The Old One had often told Caitlin how Tormod Rudh had seen the Sluagh on the night Morag had died. And now it had come back to carry away the spirit of the Old One.

Caitlin turned and ran, leaving the precious meat scattered on the ground—an unexpected feast for scavenging gulls and crows. She headed straight down the hill and then followed the crumbling sheep path along the cliff's edge. A ewe and its lamb skittered out of her way in a shower of loose gravel. Only when she reached the marsh at the bottom of the meadow did she slow down. Then on across the Big Stream, over the dyke, and up to the little house on Oiseval. When she burst inside she was astonished to find the Old One muttering to herself as she stirred a pot of stew over the peat fire.

"I thought—I thought something had happened to you," Caitlin gasped, tears of relief streaming down her cheeks. "When I was up on Ruaival, I saw the Sluagh and . . ."

The Old One raised her hand to stop the flow of Caitlin's words.

"Hush, child!" she said. "Someone's coming."

The following day, the white-clad druids led the funeral procession from the house on Oiseval to the Place of the Dead on Mullach Geal, walking deasil following the sun's shadow, walking the way of the druids. Caitlin and the Old One walked together, immediately behind the coffin bearers. The keening wail of the other mourners completely drowned out the girl's dry sobs. It was strange how she'd been crying tears of relief at finding the Old One safe when Gareth came with the news of Tormod Rudh's death, yet she had not been able to cry real tears since.

Gareth had stumbled into the house, his weather-beaten face gray with horror, and told them that Tormod Rudh had fallen from near the top of Conochair all the way to the sea, a thousand feet below. Gareth had been holding the rope and swore that it had been cut through by druid magic. Tormod was too skilled a climber to lose his footing, and a section of rope had still been tied to him when he fell.

The sea hadn't given up Tormod Rudh's body—for that was the way of the sea—and the empty coffin was an added grief. The druids said that the coffin was always empty, even when the body was there, because the spirit had already gone to its true resting place on the rocks of Mullach Bi or below the springs of Ruaival or in a dark cave on Conochair. It would have comforted Caitlin to know her father's resting place, but only the Stallir knew that. And only he could summon the spirits back from the rocks and stones and caves.

The procession wound slowly up through the heather and encircled the open grave to wait for the shadow of the hill to reach the burial stone, as was the custom. The women were still keening and wailing, while the druids stood as impassive as the granite rock.

Although the day was hot, Caitlin shivered inside her sheepskin cloak. It seemed that all the heat in the sun could never warm her blood again. She leaned against the Old One, who in turn leaned on her twisted cane. Across the circle Dougal, dazed and white-faced, presented such an image of suffering that Caitlin felt a rush of anger, and that was better than grief. What right had Dougal to stand there looking as if his own father had gone over the cliff?

Caitlin raised her eyes and saw that the Stallir was standing directly behind Dougal. He had thrown back his hood, revealing his sun-bleached hair, and the eyes staring back at Caitlin were icy blue. There was something in his long, hard look that made Caitlin unable to turn away. Her breath came in short, stabbing gasps, as if she were drowning in his strange blue eyes. She felt herself pass from light to dark and back to light again. The keening of the women all around her became one with the screaming of the fulmars and gannets and herring gulls riding the winds on the heights of Conochair.

Tormod Rudh was poised on the edge of the cliff. Caitlin could see him clearly, his long pliable fowling rod in his hand and his climbing rope knotted around his waist. Dougal was there, too, carefully looping the rope around a spur of rock. And Gareth and Neil Mor to hold the rope. Caitlin felt Tormod's exultation as he lowered himself over the edge, his feet groping for cracks and holds that no eye could detect. He knew this section of the cliff with his whole body. Leaning outward so that the rope took his weight, he signaled to Dougal to follow. Now both of them were suspended above the ocean, so far above it that the eternal movement of the waves seemed fixed. Tormod scared a bird from a crevice, and Dougal snared it as it rose into the air. A deft snap of the neck and then the head was tucked under Dougal's belt, leaving his hands free to play the fowling rod again.

Suddenly Tormod's head jerked back and he looked upward. He could have been checking Dougal's catch because his own belt was almost full, but his eye was fixed on the rope some distance above Dougal's head. Caitlin's heartbeat quickened, seeing the rope through Tormod's eyes. It was badly frayed, and while she watched, another strand parted. The rope could not hold the weight of the man and the lad for the time it would take for Gareth and Neil to pull them to safety—but it might bear the weight of a boy alone. Tormod bellowed to the men on the top of the cliff to pull them home, at the same time reaching for his cutting stone and drawing it across the rope between himself and Dougal.

Now Caitlin saw the scene through Dougal's eyes. The tautness of the rope above him and the lifeless drifting of the rope swinging loose below. The men dragged Dougal over the lip of the cliff. By the time the lad turned around and peered over the edge, Tormod's body had been claimed by the waves. But

34

Dougal saw the jagged shelf of rock stained red. Then the white foam broke again and washed it clean. Sickness rose in his throat.

Caitlin too felt the acid taste of bile on her tongue. The pain of witnessing her father's death emptied her mind, but gradually other thoughts seeped in. She tried to fight them because it was easier to feel nothing, but then the realization that Tormod Rudh had died a hero's death took hold. Gareth had hidden her father's bravery under rumors of the druid dark magic. He would use Tormod's death to stir up more hatred, when instead he should be telling of it in the druid way of poetry and song. Without the fabric of words to preserve it, Tormod's gift of life to Dougal would never be known, never be remembered. The skill of the climbers on the cliffs kept their bodies alive, but music and words could keep their deeds alive long after they were laid in the dark place on Mullach Geal and their spirits had become part of the island. This was surely what Morag had wanted when she spoke of the islanders and the druids becoming one people. The islanders needed the skill of words and music as much as the druids needed a share of the harvest.

The hollow sound of a clod of earth falling against the coffin brought Caitlin back to the Place of the Dead. The shadow had at last reached the burial stone. Caitlin's voice joined the Old One's in a trembling wail, and the men heaped stones and turf in a great mound over the empty coffin.

5
ᏟHE DARK DAYS

DRUAG'S YOUNGEST DAUGHTER Sine and her husband
Barra and their two children had moved in with
Caitlin and the Old One, but even four extra people—
five after Sine's new babe was born—could not fill the
empty place left by Tormod Rudh. For Caitlin the
winter dragged even more than usual. She kept wishing for the sun to come back so that she could get
outside and climb the crags of Dun or snare puffins on
the grassy slopes on Ruaival, but then she would
remember that her father would not lead the way, and
her eyes would flood with tears.

The Old One and Sine kept busy making sinew
snares or tanning hides. They chided Caitlin for her
idleness, although Caitlin wasn't idle when she
crouched over the fire, staring at the flickering pictures
in the glowing peat. She was seeing the heroism of
Tormod's death and wishing for the skill to put it into
words. She thought, too, about the Stallir, and how he

had sent the picture into her mind on the day of her father's funeral. That was surely a magic worth knowing. But if she ever tried to turn the talk to the druids, the others silenced her, even though they spoke of the druids themselves.

"Two of them came over from Gleann Mor yesterday," Barra announced one morning after he had come back from the shore with a handful of shellfish. He shook the rain out of his hair and rough black beard. "They took some fulmar meat from Neil Mor's storage cleit—as if we didn't give them enough at the Samain feast!"

"When they come again all the cleits will be empty, and you know what'll happen then," Sine whispered, drawing her little ones close.

"Maybe the gannets will return early," the Old One said.

"But if they don't . . ."

"Hush, Sine! Hush!"

One of the children whimpered.

"I wish the wind would drop, and then we could take the boat over to Boreray and bring back a few sheep," Barra said.

"Leaving me a widow when another storm blows in," Sine rejoined sharply. "No man in his right mind goes out in the boat before the birds are back."

Caitlin stopped listening. She'd heard all this before. But the words of her poem wouldn't come when her ears ached from the whining of the wind and her stomach hurt from hunger. She wanted to get outside, to cross the island . . . to listen to Feadair again. She saw the druids in her mind, seated in Armunna's House, the magic flame playing on their shadowed faces as they listened to the music of the harp and the seer took them to other times and other places. To have the gift of seeing with other eyes beyond one's own time and place! Caitlin reached into the pouch dangling from her belt and clasped the token that Morag had given her. As the roughness dug into her hand it almost seemed that she could hear the music of the druid's harp in the winds wailing and trembling outside the door.

As the winter wore on even Sine gave up any pretense of work. Late one afternoon, when all of them were irritable from hunger and boredom, a sudden hammering at the door roused them. Barra jumped to his feet and undid the bolt. The next minute Morda and Dougal burst inside, and Morda began telling them about the fierceness of the storm in a high, excited voice.

"We crawled up Oiseval from one rock to the next, roped together as if we were on the face of the cliff!" she said.

"What was Rona thinking of, letting you come in a storm like this?" the Old One asked.

"Dougal wanted to come," Morda answered. "He wouldn't take no for an answer, and I couldn't stand another day of hearing them wonder when the storm is going to blow itself out and when the birds will return. . . ."

"You'll hear the same talk here," Caitlin warned, though she knew Morda would be content with Sine's new baby to fuss over.

"We've nothing to offer you except some boiled dulse and a few mussels," the Old One said. "But sit down and warm yourself. You too, lad!"

Dougal was standing by the door, with an expression that reminded Caitlin of Gorm the sheepdog when it wanted to come in by the fire. Dougal spent a long time taking off his cloak, then crouched near Caitlin, though there was room by Barra closer to the fire. Caitlin couldn't think of a thing to say that hadn't to do with food or the storm. Finally Dougal broke the silence.

"I came to tell you what they're saying about you . . . and your father's death," he said.

"About *me*? What can they be saying about me?" Caitlin asked in surprise.

"That you bring bad luck . . . that you called down the Sluagh."

"To take my own father?"

"You—you know how it is during the dark days," Dougal stammered. "People look for someone to blame. . . . I just wanted to warn you . . . not to give them reason."

"They'd be nearer the truth if they blamed you,"

Caitlin said sharply. "Did you never think that Tormod might have cut the rope between himself and you because the rope was fraying? My father gave his life so that Gareth and Neil could bring you home safe."

"That could be," Dougal answered slowly. "I looked at the rope afterward. It was severed clean, yet there was a frayed part farther up. But don't go telling people that, Caitlin. They'd only wonder how you knew."

Dougal looked curiously at Caitlin, as if he too were wondering, but she didn't answer his unspoken question. She was thinking that even if she did find the words to describe Tormod's bravery, she'd never be able to share them with the islanders as long as there was so much superstition and fear.

"They recall that the Spirit Host was seen before your mother Morag's death as well," Dougal continued.

"But I was only a baby then!" Caitlin protested.

"Next they'll be dragging up the old story that you were a changeling child," the Old One said from the other side of the fire pit.

"And they whisper that it's your fault that the birds are late this spring."

"When the sun returns and the birds are nesting on the cliffs, all this will be forgotten," the Old One assured them. "It's the same every year."

Caitlin hoped the old woman was right. She no longer had Tormod Rudh to provide for her. And if the islanders were whispering that she brought bad luck, they might not ask the Old One to preside at a birth or attend a sickbed, and the storage cleit would not be full at Samain when the druids demanded a share of the harvest.

6
BLESSING THE TOBAR WELL

ON BELTANE MORNING Caitlin crept out of the house just before the sun came up. Soaring birds wove a pattern against the dawn, and the sky was clear, except for a cap of mist resting on Conochair. Beltane was a time for new beginnings—unfolding buds and hatching eggs—a season of joy. Happiness broke through her grief and worry, as unexpected as the pale-yellow primroses shining in the thick grass along the stream.

Later in the day, Caitlin was part of the crowd going up Ruaival to the well. As she slowed her pace to match that of the Old One, who crept slowly up the worn track, her fingers tightened around her gift, feeling the familiar cold roughness of it. They were all taking gifts to the well—a fragment of cloth to tie to the rowan bush or a colored pebble to toss into the water—to ensure that the spring would keep running cold and pure. Caitlin knew that it was going to be hard to part with her mother's gift, yet she couldn't escape the conviction that this was what Morag wanted her to do. If the gift was worthy, the spirits sometimes answered from the well. She'd never heard her mother speak—only her mother's words distilled in other voices. Surely if she gave the token to the well, Morag's spirit would ask her what she wanted in return. Caitlin reached out a steadying hand to help the Old One while others hurried past them. They were still struggling up the last slope when the druids began their slow walk around the pool, chanting the blessing. Three times around the well, walking deasil, the way of the sun, the way of the seasons, the way of the druids.

"They've already started!" Caitlin said.

"Let them do their part," the Old One answered, making no attempt to hurry.

The druids had finished circling the well and now stood as motionless as stones. The islanders had to pass them to present their gifts. Even the smallest children were quiet, for they had been told that the spirit voices were thin and high and could not be heard over the sound of human speech. Leaving the Old One's side, Caitlin stepped forward, clutching the token so tightly that it bit into the palm of her hand. For a moment she hesitated. Then she tossed it into the pool. She watched it spiral down through the clear water until it settled on the bottom, a golden crumpled oak leaf among the pebbles. She stood very still, but could hear only the whisper of the wind and the crying of the birds on the cliffs. The happiness she'd discovered earlier that morning seemed to fade around the edges. She'd been so sure that this was what Morag had wanted her to do.

When Caitlin turned to go, she saw that in her eagerness to present her gift she had stepped between Feadair and the Stallir without even noticing them. They were looking beyond her, staring down into the depths of the well. Although no word was spoken aloud, Caitlin felt something pass between them. Her heart began to race, and she knew how the struggling fulmar feels when the noose tightens on its neck—but there was nothing holding her. She turned and ran straight down the steep side of Ruaival, not taking the time to follow the winding path. She was almost at the bottom when she saw a white-cloaked druid immediately in front of her, blocking her way. It was Feadair, though Caitlin didn't see how he could have overtaken her.

"The gift, my child, you had the gift!"

"I gave the gift . . . I gave it to the well," she stammered.

"Where did you get it?" he asked.

Afraid to meet his eyes, Caitlin found herself studying his hands. His fingers were very long, and the cuffs of his white cloak were dirty.

"Who gave you the token?"

"It was my mother's," she whispered.

"And your mother's name was Morag?"

44

Caitlin nodded.

"And they call you . . . ?"

"Caitlin."

"What do you expect from us in return for the token you gave to the well, Caitlin?"

Caitlin's heart was hammering again, but because she'd thought so much about the druid gift of poetry and song during the dark days, she knew what she wanted. "I'd like to be able to put my thoughts into words that sing," she whispered. "I want people to remember Tormod Rudh."

"Tormod Rudh?"

"He was my father. He—he went over the cliff last summer . . ."

Feadair reached out and took Caitlin's hands, folding them in his. "Meet me by the stone circle on the height of Conochair as the sun sinks into the western sea, that the gift may be yours. . . ."

And then he was gone.

Caitlin didn't see him go. Maybe he had the gift of disappearing. Or perhaps he hadn't been there at all. Una's brothers Gair and Callum were scuffling in the heather not far ahead of her. They wouldn't be doing that if a druid were near.

Later in the day, while Caitlin was down on the beach helping Sine and Rona stack heather and discarded thatch for the Beltane fire, the encounter with Feadair still filled her thoughts. She wondered if she really had

45

seen him—or had it only been his likeness in a druid sending? What would happen if she did meet him by the stones on Conochair? Shadows of dark magic hovered on the edge of her mind, but she pushed them away. The tall druid's voice had been gentle. What had he meant when he said that the gift would be hers?

"Staring at the pile won't make it grow, Caitlin," Rona said sharply.

Caitlin sighed and set off to fetch another load. Una and Beitris were on their way down from the village empty-handed and were so busy discussing who they hoped would ask them to jump the Beltane fire that they didn't notice Caitlin. Hearing them giggling together suddenly made her angry. All the girls would have boys to dance with around the fire . . . and no one was going to choose her.

On her way back down with the next load, she saw that Beitris and Una were now chasing after Neil Beag. When they finally caught him, they used a ribbon of kelp to tie him up in the cage of whale ribs that had been on the beach for as long as Caitlin could remember. They were all screaming with laughter.

"I reckon he didn't try to get away!"

The unexpected voice made Caitlin jump. Dougal, with a bundle of thatch for the fire, fell into step beside her. Caitlin plodded along in moody silence, stopping to shift her bundle every now and again. When Dougal spoke again, his words took her completely by surprise.

"Caitlin, will you leap the Beltane fire with me tonight?" he asked abruptly.

For a moment Caitlin thought he must be teasing. Asking her to leap the fire was as good as saying that they would be wed, and she had never given him reason to think that! She was so agitated that part of her bundle of thatch slipped sideways. Trying to grab it, she lost most of the rest. A gust of wind caught the straw, sending it in all directions, which matched her thoughts. Dougal was only asking her because she'd told him that Tormod Rudh had saved his life . . . and he needn't imagine that jumping the Beltane fire could somehow even that score. Or maybe he was asking her because he knew that no one else would. She didn't need pity. Not from him or anyone! To think that she'd been worrying that no one would ask her, and now—Dougal.

Dougal had set his bundle down to help Caitlin collect her straw, but his straw began blowing about too. Caitlin snatched up all she could carry and rushed off.

"I'll look for you at the fire tonight," Dougal shouted breathlessly.

Caitlin ran on without answering. Dougal could look all he wanted—but he wouldn't find her! Tonight, when the Beltane fire was burning, she'd be with Feadair at the stone circle on the heights of Conochair. At least now the decision was easy!

7

CATHAN

TWO ANGRY SKUAS wheeled around Caitlin's head, darting at her face with loud, scolding cries. They were only afraid for their nest, but it wasn't hard to believe they wanted her to turn back. The wind, too, was pushing against her, tugging at her long red-gold hair and molding her gray shift to her slender body. The sun was disappearing fast as Caitlin drew near the place on Conochair where the cliffs dropped into the sea, but she could make out the druid stones quite clearly. Her heart pounded as she counted them. Twelve standing stones leaning into the wind, and one laid flat. Caitlin was just beginning to think that she had come all that way for nothing—and she wasn't altogether sorry—when a figure emerged from between two of the stones and came gliding toward her.

"I wasn't sure you'd come," the druid said quietly.

Caitlin looked up at Feadair, meeting his dark gaze. The words, implying uncertainty, made her bold.

"I thought the druids knew everything," she answered.

"And would *you* like to know everything?"

"I told you that I want to be able to put my thoughts into words that sing," she said. Feadair's eyes were as black as the water in Childa Well, and Caitlin had the uncanny feeling that it would be easy to drown in those strange eyes. "I want to know what lies beyond—to know other people and to hear other voices."

"So little?" Feadair asked, his voice mocking her. "You would have the power of the bard and the seer, both! But you are right, child. Before the words will come, you must see what lies beyond . . . the connections . . . the way one thing touches on another. The gift of words is empty without the gift of seeing . . . without the understanding that a chance meeting shapes eternity . . . a deed undone, a word unspoken, leaves a black hole in the fabric of our lives. But to understand completely, you need the courage to reach outside yourself . . . to go forward . . . to see how what we do now affects the time that will be. . . ."

Feadair's final words were lost in the harsh cries of the birds coming home to roost on the cliffs. The sun had dropped into the sea. In her mind Caitlin saw the four small islands—Hirta, Soay, Boreray, and Dun— shrink to nothing as darkness wrapped the world. There was no escaping the dark. The smallness of the islands, set in the vastness of the sea, reminded her of

Feadair's song about a time when there had been no water between Hirta and the land on the far horizon. People had walked back and forth, making the journey as easily as the islanders walked from Village Bay to Gleann Mor. Then the rains had come, for forty days and forty nights, and the water covered the land. . . . But no . . . it had not been the bard who had told her that. That came from a story in Brendan's black book. Caitlin's thoughts were rushing forward and backward, wheeling and circling like a bird in search of its own nesting place. And then, as if she'd alighted on a familiar rock, her mind came into sharp focus.

For a moment she was startled to see bright sunshine, and she closed her eyes against it. When she opened them, she found herself alone. Feadair had vanished, and the stone circle with him. Caitlin walked cautiously over to where the stones should have been and found that they were in fact still there but now lay flat and were so overgrown that they were almost one with the wind-swept moor. How long had it taken for the creeping turf to overtake those huge stones? One hundred—two hundred—three hundred years?

And she wasn't alone after all. From where she stood, she could see four birdmen farther along the cliff, one spread-eagled against the sheer face, while the others directed him from above. She couldn't make out the rope that joined them, but she could see from the angles of the men's bodies as they braced themselves that they were working together with effortless rhythm, like birds riding the winds. The young man on the rock face maneuvered his fowling rod toward a shelf where several fulmars perched. Some of the birds were wary and had taken to the air, but the lad deftly dropped the noose over a sitting bird's head. The rod jerked in his hand, the men above leaned back from the cliff, holding the rope taut, and the lad's foot skidded. Caitlin's heart skidded too.

"Iain," she breathed. "Take care, lad, take care!" Iain steadied himself and added the bird to the others hanging from his belt. Now she had time to wonder how she'd known his name. But what was there to wonder about? She had known Iain Briagh all her life. She knew his name as well as she knew her own name was Cathan. Uncertainty flickered again at the edge of her mind, but she pushed it away. Was she not up here looking for tormentil root, when there was plenty closer to her house, because she'd known that Iain was birding on Conochair? But she really should be on her way home. She'd promised the old grandmother that she'd help with the oat harvest.

The girl ran lightly along the sheep's track that skirted the cliffs. She loved this view of the ocean, so far below that the water looked as smooth as the Tobar pool with the wheeling birds drifting like feathers on its surface. When she reached the Gap, she stopped to catch her breath, then blinked and rubbed her eyes. A boat was heading toward Hirta from Boreray. Hovering above it was what seemed to be a huge colored blanket. She watched the strange vessel with a mixture of fear and fascination until it disappeared behind the headland of Oiseval. Then, oblivious to the scratches on her long brown legs, she raced through the heather to bring this amazing news down to the village.

"A boat!" she screamed. "A boat full of people is coming over the sea from Boreray!"

The grandmother, in the middle of the oat field, where the grain was heavy-headed and golden, didn't hear Cathan. She stooped to pull another plant, lifting it by the roots to get the full length of straw and then shaking the soil back into the earth, all the while being careful not to lose any seeds. But the old woman's husband Fergus heard. He had been napping, and came hobbling around the side of the house to see what the excitement was about. Before Cathan had finished telling Fergus exactly what she'd seen, the boat rounded the headland, breasting the waves like a majestic seabird. The blanket above the boat, striped red and white, billowed out like a woman in her ninth month and seemed to pull the boat toward the shore. By this time the grandmother had left her harvesting and joined Cathan and Fergus.

"Surely it must be God who is coming to visit," the old woman said, shading her bright black eyes with a wrinkled hand.

"Nay, I do not think it is God," Fergus said slowly.

They could now make out a figure carved on the prow, a grotesque, horned creature painted yellow and black, with red eyes and a gaping red mouth. Some of the villagers had run down to meet the boat, but they stopped at the edge of the shingle, afraid to go closer.

"I stood upon the sand of the sea and saw a beast rise up out of the sea, having seven heads and ten horns, and upon his horns ten crowns, and upon his heads the name of blasphemy." The words from the ancient black book came readily to Fergus's lips.

"I think, in truth, it is the devil who comes," the grandmother whispered, her voice shaking. "Let's get away from here."

The old woman grabbed the girl's arm and they scuttled back to the doorway of the house on Oiseval, where they stood together wide-eyed and silent as the boat came toward the beach. Before it reached the shore, about twenty men leaped out and plunged through the waist-deep water. Their hoarse shouting, shining shields, glittering spears, and helmets horned like Soay sheep struck terror into the heart of every person watching. Those who had ventured down to the shore scattered like mice running from the shadow of a hovering eagle, then peered from behind stacks of peat or through the chinks in the walls of the storage cleits at the tide of men streaming up the beach.

The strangers paid no heed to the people but made straight for the sheep grazing in the pasture close to the Big Stream. Yelling and cheering, they struck them down, butchering the harmless beasts with no respect for their bodies or their spirits. Druce, old Fergus's faithful sheepdog, charged a bearded man with golden hair and teeth as white as bleached shells. The man lifted his arm, about to hurl his spear at Druce, but Fergus had raised Druce from a pup and couldn't stand by and see the brave dog's life cut short. He stumbled out from behind the rock where he had been cowering and ran between Druce and the man. The spear meant for the dog pierced Fergus's heart. The man, who looked like a god, was surely kin to the devil.

With a sharp, frightened cry, the girl buried her face against the old grandmother's thin shoulder. Deep inside her terror was the agony that she had somehow brought these things to pass. If she could just get away, this wouldn't be happening.

"Cathan, Cathan!" the old woman crooned, holding her close.

Cathan. The way the name sounded on the grandmother's tongue anchored the frightened girl to the present.

"Who are they, Grandmother?" she whispered. "Where have they come from?"

"They are Vikings, Cathan, and they come from a land far north of Boreray."

Vikings! Cathan had heard the word whispered by the hearth on a winter's night, though it was rarely spoken aloud if there were children near. She could at last understand the fear and the silence.

From their hiding places around the village and up on the hill, the Hirtans watched everything the Vikings did. One group dragged the boat onto the shore, apparently knowing the way of the tides and changing winds in Village Bay, where an anchored boat could be torn from its moorings and splintered on the rocks of Dun. They unloaded a huge cooking pot and cups and bowls and more things than Cathan could name. Others went off in search of fuel and then built a roaring fire to cook the slaughtered ewes. Toward evening, tent frames were set up in the lee of Oiseval and covered with striped cloth. The boards at the gable ends of the frame had been carved into animal heads and painted like the animal on the prow of the ship. Cathan decided that the strange carvings must be to protect the invaders while they slept, but they didn't need protection on Hirta. The islanders lived by the words Brendan had taught them long ago: *Be not forgetful to entertain strangers; for thereby some have entertained angels unawares.* But this time they were entertaining devils.

When darkness fell, the Hirtans crept out of Village Bay and made their way over the pass to Gleann Mor. And there they found that the Vikings had done something that was perhaps even more terrible than killing Fergus. They had hacked down the sacred oak trees that had been growing on the island since the beginning of time. They had felled the last trees, the trees which harbored the spirits of the druid fathers.

Although the night was mild, the islanders crowded into Armunna's House. They were afraid to be outdoors with the ghosts of the druids roaming the hills now that the trees were gone. Gradually, as everyone settled for the night, the anxious talk subsided, leaving only the voice of young Seumas, the harpist. Cathan, lying close to her brothers and sisters, listened to his sad refrain:

> "They felled the last trees,
> The home of our fathers.
> They felled the last trees
> To burn in their fire."

Suddenly Cathan sat up and looked around. "Where's Grandmother?" she asked.

"She stayed behind," her mother answered. "To be with Fergus."

"You should have made her come!"

"She had to do what had to be done," Cathan's mother said gently.

The next morning, before the sun was up, Iain and his friends Coll and Marcus were talking together about going over to Village Bay to find out what was happening.

"Can I go with you?" Cathan asked. "I want to make sure that Grandmother's safe."

"You'd better stay here," Iain said, pulling his heavy

sheepskin cloak over his shoulders. "We're going to creep up on the village, crawling down through the heather like sheep."

"But that's stupid!" Cathan exclaimed. "It was the sheep they were after yesterday. You'd be better off without cloaks!"

Iain scowled. "How would you have us go?" he asked angrily. "Marching right up to them as targets for their spears?"

"A covering of mud would be better protection than a sheepskin," Cathan retorted.

"She's right," Coll agreed, throwing down his cloak. "I'd sooner travel light so that I can run. And if it comes to running, Cathan's faster than any of us!"

So Cathan went with them, though at first Iain pretended she wasn't there. Knowing, as they did, every rock and outcrop on the hill, they had no trouble reaching one of the storage cleits above the village without being seen. From there they watched the Vikings through chinks in the wall.

"They're packing up," Coll said.

"Aye, and they've done this before," Iain whispered bitterly. "See how they work together."

The boat had been pushed partway into the water, and a broad plank connected it to the beach. Some of the men were storing meat under the floorboards, while others folded the tents and gathered up cooking pots and bowls and blankets. Cathan felt sick with rage watching them strut about the beach shouting and laughing as if Hirta belonged to them. Finally every-thing was loaded. The last few men pushed the boat free of the sand and were dragged aboard by their cheering companions. Cathan didn't leave the cleit until the sail had caught the wind, carrying the boat far out into the bay.

Iain, Coll, and Marcus ran down to the beach to scavenge, but Cathan headed for the grandmother's house up on Oiseval. By the flickering light of the fulmar oil lamp she saw the old woman sitting on the earthen floor beside Fergus's body stretched out in the sleeping crub. During the night, she must have half-carried, half-dragged him home. The night watch had been long and lonely, but now that the old woman could give voice to her grief, her keening, mourning cry filled the room.

That same day, they carried Fergus up to the Place of the Dead. The funeral procession followed the path of the sun's shadow in the way that the druids had led them long ago. While they waited for the shadow to reach the funeral stone, their weeping was not just for Fergus, whose spirit was now safe in the rocks and streams of Hirta, but for the shame that one man had taken another's life. Donald Mac Ghillie pronounced that from that day on, no one must ever step on the spot where Fergus's blood had stained the heather. And so it would be, even after the reason for walking around the place was long forgotten.

After the burial they went up to the little church on Ruaival. Cathan sat by the old grandmother, sharing her wool cloak, although with so many crowded in together there was no need for it. The flap of stretched skin that served as a door had been thrown back so that those who were left outside could hear. Donald Mac Ghillie recited the words from the black book, and everyone joined in, their voices soaring up to the bleached-bone rafters.

> "I will lift up my eyes to the
>   hills, from whence cometh my help.
> My help cometh from the Lord
>   which made heaven and earth.
> The sun shall not smite thee by
>   day, nor the moon by night.
> The Lord shall preserve thee from
>   all evils: He shall preserve thy soul.
> The Lord shall preserve thy going
>   out and thy coming in from this time
>   forth, and even for evermore."

When the singing and stories were ended, Cathan and the old woman went back to gathering the grain from the trampled oat field. It didn't seem possible to Cathan that she'd seen the boat off Boreray only yesterday. It troubled her to discover that the whole world could change between one sunrise and the next and nothing she did made any difference . . . though if

she'd stayed home yesterday and helped the grandmother, there would at least have been more grain in
the storage cleit. More food for the coming winter.
Tears streamed down her face.

"Run along, lassie!" the old woman said kindly. "Go
and see what the Vikings left behind. And dry those
tears or you won't find much!"

A crowd of men, women, and children were busy
scouring the ground where the Vikings had camped.
Some of them had found metal tools—a good knife and
a chisel among them—and a ladle and even a cooking
pot. Cathan picked up a bronze brooch with a blood-
red stone in it. It was beautiful. But she remembered
old Fergus and hurled it into the sea. She wanted no
part of the Viking kind.

8
SEASON OF FEAR

CATHAN STOOD IN the doorway, soaking up the sunshine. The sky was brilliant blue and the soft breeze rippled the purple moor grass, but the birds were not yet nesting on the cliffs and the storage cleits were empty. Her brothers and sisters had gone out to play, still hungry after a scant meal of boiled dulse and whey milk. There had been no need to wash the cooking pot because it had already been wiped clean.

The men were sitting on the dyke talking about going over to Boreray to catch gannets. Although the wind had died, the waves still thundered up the beach and showered the rocks of Dun with spray. Some thought the sea was too rough and others wanted to work on the boat before risking it on such a sea. The discussion looked as if it was going to last all morning, but then Cathan's father said that he for one was going to chance the weather and the boat for the sake of fresh meat in the pot. Now the talk turned to who should go and who should stay. Cathan could only catch snatches of it, but when Iain grinned and slapped his hands together, she guessed that he was included.

After the boat was launched, it was hard to settle down to anything. Hirta always seemed empty when anyone was gone to the other islands. The men wouldn't be back before the following day at the earliest because gannets were hunted at night while they roosted on the cliffs.

"Missing that lad of yours?" the old grandmother asked Cathan with a sly grin.

Cathan pretended not to hear.

"Some of the girls went up to the Gap to look for a signal from Boreray, Cathan. Run and you'll catch up with them."

If there were problems on Boreray—an accident or a wreck—the men let those at home know by turning over a patch of turf on the hillside facing Hirta. As long as the pasture was green, everything was going well.

"Do you want to come?" Cathan asked.

The grandmother shook her head. "I was over in Gleann Mor this morning at the ewe milking and that's enough for these old bones in one day."

Cathan noticed how weary the old woman looked.

"If we brought the sheep back to the meadow by the Big Stream, you wouldn't have to walk so far," Cathan said.

"There's good grass at Gleann Mor," the grandmother answered. "Besides, the enclosure in front of

Armunna's House is a fine place for the early lambs
and for the milking."

But that wasn't the only reason the sheep had been
driven to the far side of the island. While she walked
up the rough track on Oiseval, Cathan was thinking
that fear of the Vikings clung like smoke after the fire
was out. On Hirta, where life was dangerous, they
lived with fear, but this being afraid of people was a
different kind of fear. A fear that never went away,
even when the cause of it was gone. And it divided
them. Coll and Iain wanted to build a fortress instead
of more storage cleits, and during the winter some of
the men had made clubs instead of new digging tools,
even though the black book said that wisdom is better
than weapons of war.

By the time Cathan reached the Gap, the wind had
lost its softness. It tugged at her hair and stung her
cheeks. She joined a group of laughing girls clustered
around her cousin Fiona, not even needing to glance
across at Boreray to tell that the hillside facing Hirta
was green.

But then the laughter died.

Seana had caught everyone's attention and was
pointing at something. Squinting down at the ocean,
Cathan saw a boat, level with the sharp outline of the
tall rock they called Stac Lee. The boat changed
course and the square sail took on the crescent shape of
the new moon. The girls talked together in frightened
whispers, not daring to take their eyes off the sea.

Someone said the boat was too low in the water for a Viking ship, but Fiona pointed out that it had the same high prow as the one that had come before.

"We've got to stop them," Cathan burst out.

"There's nothing we can do," Seana said.

And Cathan knew that Seana was right. After one last look at the boat, they started down the hill to bring the dreaded news to the village.

Decisions were made on Hirta by talking the matter out, each man having his say. This was how they always settled quarrels and how they divided the fields and the nesting areas of the cliffs according to each family's need. When the matter wasn't urgent, the discussion often lasted all day. But today, with a Viking boat rounding the headland and the ablest men away on Boreray, the old customs didn't hold.

The grandmother spoke up. "It was their coming the first time that brought the harm," she said, looking out beyond the circle of fearful faces. "Taking my man's life. Trampling the oats and killing the sheep. Aye, the worst is done. Perhaps this time they have come to put right the wrong."

"I think we should all go over to Gleann Mor and see to the sheep," Donald Mac Ghillie suggested quietly.

Several people nodded, liking the idea. That way it didn't sound as if they were running away from the Vikings. A few women went off to gather up cooking pots and woolen cloaks and sheepskins, while their men fetched ropes and snares and the scraps of meat left in the storage cleits.

"If they're coming for more sheep, it would be better for them to find the sheep here in Village Bay than to follow us to Gleann Mor in search of them," Seana pointed out.

"We can let a few wander back in this direction," Donald answered.

"For the Vikings to kill?" Cathan asked, horrified.

"What do a few sheep matter?" Donald retorted. "So long as the birds come back to Hirta each spring, we need ask for nothing more."

"But if the Vikings also come each year . . ." Cathan's mother wailed, the future of her six children heavy on her mind. "Why couldn't things have stayed the way they were before the boat came like a beast rising up from the sea?"

"Where's your faith, woman?" Donald asked roughly. "We are made of granite, born to endure. These Vikings hide cowardly hearts behind metal shields. They wave iron spears because they have no strength in their hands. Can you see one of them swinging down from the heights of Conochair or scaling the straight walls of Stac Lee?"

Donald's words helped ease the pain. Cathan and her mother bundled up their belongings in sheepskin blankets and hid what they couldn't carry in one of the cleits farthest from the bay. Alasdair, the oldest boy, was told to take the loom.

"The Vikings'll be gone long before the sheep lose their wool!" he protested.

"If we only knew . . ."

They set off in a straggling group, the women bent double under their heavy loads. The littlest ones ran alongside, jumping and jostling one another and chasing the dogs. After being cooped up all winter, it was hard for them not to find joy in the expedition to Gleann Mor in the sunshine.

Cathan walked with her mother, going slowly so as not to leave the grandmother and old Donald Mac Ghillie too far behind. At the top of the pass they paused to look back at the snug turf-roofed houses in the valley and the old church up on Ruaival. Already the village had a desolate, deserted look, but maybe it was just knowing that there was no one there. The boat had passed the headland and they watched in silence as it changed course and turned into the bay. They could make out the colors of the red and white sail and see that it was crowded with more people than were needed for the oars. Although Cathan was anxious to be hidden away in Gleann Mor, she felt she couldn't drop down over the pass until she'd seen the strangers reach the shore. This time they landed without shouting, without spears, without horned helmets. A few men came first, cautiously exploring the whole area of Village Bay. Then came the rest, womenfolk as well as men. And sheep, and beasts bigger than sheep that carried the loads up from the beach. Tents and tools and utensils.

"I wish our men had not gone to Boreray," Cathan's mother said, repeating the words the women had been saying all afternoon like a mournful litany.

"They'll have seen the boat pass the island," the old grandmother assured her. "And they'll see our fires on Gleann Mor. They'll find us there."

"If these people have come to stay, when will we go back to Village Bay?"

No one had the answer to that.

"Aye, it could be that settlers may hurt us more than warriors," Donald Mac Ghillie said.

Cathan picked up her bundle and trudged down the hill. No matter what Donald thought, she was glad that this time the Vikings hadn't come with spears and helmets.

When Cathan's family reached Armunna's House, it was so crowded with people and their belongings that they went off to look for someplace else to spend the night. Cathan and Alasdair led the way to a big cleit up on the Cambir, overlooking Gleann Bay. Long ago, when the druids had lived in Armunna's House, they must have used these huge cleits for storing their food. The druid fathers were only a memory now, preserved in words and songs, but the underground house and the storage cleits had endured.

The following morning Cathan's family found that they'd have been better off in the cramped quarters of Armunna's House after all. As so often happened after a spell of mild weather in early spring, another storm had blown in. The cleit had a thick turf roof, but the walls were made so that the wind whistled between the stones to keep food and ropes and skins from moldering in the winter's damp. The little ones were crying and whining. They wanted to go home.

"Perhaps the Vikings could tell a storm was coming and are just taking shelter on Hirta," Cathan's mother suggested hopefully. "When the wind drops, they'll go to the sea again. Till then, we must find a way to stay warm."

Cathan and Alasdair set to work pushing clumps of turf into the spaces in the walls, but even though they spent the entire day at it, the wind still searched out the chinks and howled and screamed so that no one could sleep that night. With no fuel to feed the fire, there was no cooking the following day—only a piece of dulse to chew on. The children grew even more fretful and miserable, and their heads and ears ached from the noise of the wind.

When the storm abated a little, Alasdair ventured down to Armunna's House and brought back boiled mutton and a slab of cheese. He had heard from some of the boys that the hillside on Boreray was still green.

"Our men are likely better off than we are," the grandmother said. "They'll be in the Stallir House." She was having trouble chewing the tough mutton, for she'd lost most of her teeth. "So long as they lifted the boat out of the sea and filled it with stones before the storm struck, they'll be all right. A boat at anchor wouldn't last long in that wind."

Early the next morning they saw the Hirtan boat dipping across the water, heading directly for Gleann Bay. Cathan and Alasdair raced down to the shore. By the time the boat arrived, everyone from Armunna's House had heard the glad news. The water was stinging cold, but they all plunged into the waves to help drag the boat onto the beach.

Cathan was helping to unload the gannets the men had caught over on Boreray when Iain saw her.

"You'll freeze, lass!" he said. "Here, wrap yourself in my cloak. And tell me what's been happening. We've been frantic to get home ever since we saw the Viking boat disappear behind Oiseval."

"How did you know to come here?" Cathan asked.

"We saw the smoke from Armunna's House—and no boat, so it couldn't be the Vikings' fire."

"There's no boat in Village Bay, either!" Coll shouted. He was pleased to be first with the news. "The storm smashed it against the rocks of Dun. And some of their tents were blown clear off the island. And animals too!"

"It is as much our misfortune as theirs that they lost the boat," Donald Mac Ghillie said quietly. "How are they ever going to leave Hirta, now that they have no way of going?"

9
SEASON OF JOY

THE MEN WERE sitting along the dyke outside Armunna's House mending their ropes and snares and nets in readiness for the first hunting trip of the year. The air quivered with the noise of puffins and skuas and fulmars squabbling over nesting places on the moor and along the cliffs, but it wasn't just fresh food after a lean winter that the islanders welcomed. It was more the feeling of being part of the rhythm of life on Hirta again. Even though the Vikings had taken their snug houses and the best land, the cliffs were still theirs. A man had to be born and raised on Hirta to own the cliffs.

While the men plaited their ropes, several of the women turned over a small patch of ground for the oats they'd saved from last year's harvest. Others cut and stacked peat for fuel. It was heavy, tiring work, but they still found time to talk. And the talk was always about the Viking people. They took turns watching the strangers from hiding places on the side of Conochair above the village.

The Viking women were tall and fair, but it was their clothes that interested the Hirtans most.

"How do they make cloth the color of bluebells and roseroot?" Fiona wondered.

"And those pins that shine like the sun!"

"I wouldn't want my skirt flapping around my legs while I was working in the fields," Cathan's mother said as she added her peat to the growing stack and then went off to cut more.

Watching her mother stride bare-legged across the heath, her brown shawl secured by a bone pin at her shoulder and her skirt looped up into the cord around her waist to keep it out of her way, Cathan found herself thinking that the Viking women's clothes set them above the Hirtans somehow. They had more dignity. And they wore shoes made from animal skins shaped to their feet, while the Hirtans went barefoot— except for the few who fashioned sandals out of gannet skins, turning the skins so that the down was against their feet and their heels fitted into the neck.

The Vikings paid no heed to the islanders. They rarely went beyond Village Bay. They worked from first light until after dark, turning over land that had never been dug before, building walls around the new fields to keep the animals out. And building walls around other fields to keep the animals in. The Hirtans had never seen so much activity, though they were busy enough themselves, plucking birds and preserving them. Then they feasted for days on the tender meat of the gugas—gannets too young to fly—and eggs and fresh greens. Life on Hirta once again fell into the long-established pattern of the progressing season. A trip over to Stac Lee to collect eggs. Another expedition to Boreray to hunt the gannet. At Beltane they could not give their gifts to the Tobar Well on Ruaival, so they blessed the water in the Well of Virtues above the Gleann Burn. They lit a fire on the beach and danced away the shortest night of the year, thanking the Maker, who saw that the light was good and divided the light from the darkness. Summer was the season of joy.

For the Vikings it was the season of labor.

The task that Cathan loved most of all was gathering wool. The women pulled loose wool from the sheep's coats, but some of the plucking was done by the old heather plants that caught tufts of loose wool on their twiggy fingers. Then the girls and small children went wool gathering. The little ones usually stayed close to home, but the older girls found this a grand excuse to spy on the Vikings or to go up Conochair and watch the lads on the cliffs.

One morning, when the sun was bright and the wind had dropped to a whisper in the grass, Cathan went to look for wool on the Cambir. She knew she wouldn't find much on the smooth, thrift-covered slopes, but sheep did sometimes rest against an outcrop of rock on the grassy ridge that separated the ocean to the west from Gleann Bay on the east. The islanders called this place the Neck of Cambir. When the gray seals were singing on the rocks and skerries down below, their music drifted up, so that the voices of the seals on the west side mingled with those on the east. A person sitting on the narrowest part of the Neck could hear music that even the seals themselves couldn't hear. Cathan had once taken Iain up to the Neck, but he hadn't listened to the magic harmony. He had only wanted to look for nesting places along the cliffs.

When Cathan reached the outcrop, three sheep bleated their annoyance and ran stiff-legged back down the slope. They didn't leave any wool behind— but today the seals were singing! She sank down onto a springy cushion of thrift and settled back against a sun-soaked rock.

Soon she added her own song to the music. The words came without her having to think of them. A song about the Viking kind who had come twice from the sea and had taken everything—the sheep, the houses, the land. But the day would come when the island would belong to the Hirtans again. The seal people would lure the Vikings up Conochair with the sound of their song. The music would grow louder and higher, the Vikings running toward it. And the music would draw them on, so that they couldn't stop when they came to the edge of the land. The Viking folk would launch into the air and spread their fine clothes like the wings of birds, and they would ride the current of the wind far out to sea. Then the waves would reach up and splash their wings, making them heavy, for cloth could not shed water like feathers. And all the Vikings would sink to the bottom of the deep.

Cathan was so lost in the music of the seals and in the music of her own creation that she didn't realize until the last note died away that someone was listening to her song. One of the Vikings was sitting a little above her on the rock. Her first thought was to run, but there was nowhere to hide on the close-cropped slopes of the Cambir. Raising her arm as if to shield herself from a blow, she shrank back against the stone—but this Viking wasn't wild like the men on the beach. He began to talk to her, his voice quiet, with the soothing sound of the sentinel gannet bird when there's nothing to fear. And the strange thing was that, although he was speaking quite slowly, she couldn't understand a word he said. She lowered her arm and stared at him. It had never crossed her mind till now that there might be more than one way of talking in the world.

He smiled—a flash of white teeth—and then was solemn again. A tall, golden boy with bronze skin and light hair and eyes like the summer sky. And his clothes! Blue and green cloth, shaped to fit his arms

and legs, and fastened at the waist with a leather belt
and shining buckle. Her own wool shift was a drab
thing in comparison, and she felt slightly shamed that
it covered so little, even though it must be uncomfort-
able to be wrapped up like that on a hot day.

He wasn't in the least fierce or angry. In fact, he
seemed to be trying to sing, too, but his voice—
somewhere between boyhood and manhood—
wavered, and they both laughed. It delighted her to
discover that she knew what he was telling her, even
though she didn't understand the words. He liked the
seals' song, and he had liked her singing! That must
mean he didn't understand her words either, for he
wouldn't have liked the song if he knew that she had
just wished all his people at the bottom of the sea. To
make up for such wickedness, she reached into the
pouch tied to her belt and brought out her lunch and
held it out to him.

At the sight of the food the boy seemed to change.
He grabbed the slab of ewe cheese and crammed it into
his mouth, then ate the boiled eggs with bits of shell
still clinging to them. He was hungry, which was hard
to believe, because now that it was summer, food was
as plentiful as the birds on the cliffs. Didn't these
Vikings know how to snare puffins? She gave him all
her lunch, and then when he discovered that she had
none left for herself, he became upset.

"There are more eggs at home—more than we can
eat," Cathan said.

Now it annoyed her that she couldn't make him understand.

"Egg," she repeated, pointing to a fragment of shell. He smiled and said the word in his tongue. They both laughed again, and were soon naming everything in sight. The boy's name was Erik, though at first Cathan thought that was the name of his shirt because he pointed to it while saying Erik. Some of their words were similar, but other things seemed to have no name at all in the boy's language. He had only one word for "bird," whereas on Hirta every kind of bird had its own name and the young had different names from the grown birds.

After that first day they met quite often on Conochair or on Mullach Bi between Village Bay and Gleann Mor—though they kept well out of sight of both. Cathan had the excuse of wool gathering, while Erik pretended to be looking for eggs. Cathan usually gave him some to take home. On days when Erik didn't come, he was often working the fields. "Women's work," he called it scornfully. Men's work was fighting. But Cathan couldn't imagine Erik wearing a horned helmet or carrying a spear and shield. He wasn't like the rest.

10
SEASON OF GRIEF

THE FIRST WINTER storm came early, but the bird harvest had been good, so the cleits were well filled. There would be no hunger this year—unless the Vikings raided their stores. The worst misery was the sound of the wind whistling through the stone walls of the cleit. Cathan's family finally moved down to Armunna's House, but once they were there, Cathan found that the continuous crying of the children and squabbling among the grownups brought as much misery as the wind.

Other winters, they huddled around a peat fire, listening to stories from the black book that had come to the island long, long ago in Brendan's time. No one nowadays knew how to read the runes—perhaps no one but Brendan ever had—so they had to keep the words alive by telling them from memory, again and again, so that the children would know them and someday pass them on to their children. Already some of the words had been lost with the death of Fergus. He'd had more of the book inside his head than any of them. But this winter there was no time for stories. Instead, the men—and women, too—argued over what to do about the Vikings. Anger was never far below the surface, flaring up without warning, even among those who urged peace. Some of the boys chipped spear points from pieces of rock, while Seana's father Roderick sat hunched over the fire, fashioning a snare strong enough to choke the life out of a man.

"Violence begets violence," Donald warned him. "If we make weapons to match their weapons, the day will soon come when the only voices heard on Hirta will be the voices of the birds."

"If we don't make weapons, only Viking voices will be heard," Roderick answered bitterly.

With the first promise of spring, however, the return of the birds dominated everyone's thoughts and conversation, as it had for all the years people had lived on Hirta. One wet, blustery morning, Cathan set off to climb Mullach Bi, hoping to see the first puffin of the season. She was picking her way over a fall of rock when a low whistling cry caught her attention. It didn't match any bird call that she knew. It came again, from the direction of a tumble-down cleit farther up the hill, and this time she recognized the sound. Scrambling up to the cleit, she peered inside.

Two dark blue eyes stared back at her from a haggard face.

"Erik?" she asked uncertainly.

When the lad crawled out of the cramped cleit and unfolded himself, Cathan was dismayed to see him so thin and hungry looking. His hair no longer shone and his clothes hung loose, their bright colors stained and faded.

"I wanted to come . . . but the wind . . ." he said hoarsely.

"Are you all right?"

"We are hungry . . . always hungry . . . the rain came before the grain could be harvested."

"Have you no meat?"

"My brother's bairn died last night," Erik continued brokenly. "Astrid had no more milk."

Cathan remembered seeing Astrid last summer. A tall woman, who glowed with the joy of her coming motherhood. Cathan pushed that picture away and filled her mind instead with the words she'd been listening to around the fire all winter. Those Vikings should never have come to Hirta, taking away the peace of the island. It served them right to be hungry . . . but what about poor Astrid . . . and the bairn who'd had no say in anything? How would it all end? On so small an island, there was only room for one people.

"The birds will soon be back," Cathan said at last. "Then there'll be food enough for us all."

"We do not know your ways of catching them," Erik answered. "Oh, Cathan . . ."

Erik's words trailed off as the wind assaulted them with another burst of rain. He shivered and clutched his cloak closer about him. His hand was skin and bone like a bird's claw.

"There's meat in yon storage cleit," Cathan whispered. She pointed to a cleit on the opposite hillside, scarcely visible in the driving rain. "The one up there, farthest from Armunna's House."

As soon as the words were spoken she wished them back. The islanders were forever worrying about the Vikings raiding their stores. But surely she could trust Erik to take only what he needed to keep his people from starving. His next words reassured her.

"Bring me food. . . . Tonight, Cathan! I'll meet you up there!" He pointed to Finger Rock on Mullach Bi, where they had sometimes met last summer. He wanted to let her decide how much meat the Hirtans could spare.

"I'll get you something to eat now," she said. "Nobody's about."

"No!" Erik answered sharply. "Tonight. After it grows dark. Wait there till I come."

Cathan spent most of the long afternoon watching Iain and Marcus make sinew snares and listening to them talk about the birds they were going to catch in the summer.

"We won't be able to hunt on Dun with the Vikings down in Village Bay," Marcus said.

"The cliffs of Mullach Bi are better than Dun," Iain said.

"Not for guillemots."

"They are so, aren't they, Cathan?"

When Cathan just shrugged, Iain looked disappointed. Usually she was quick to take sides, but today she had more to worry about than the summer's hunting. For a start, one of the dogs was sniffing at the pouch of meat dangling from her waist. She should have left it outside after fetching it from the far cleit, but the dogs would have smelled it there, too. And she shouldn't have told Erik which of the cleits still had food in it. If the Vikings started helping themselves, that would lead to no end of trouble.

Across the room Seumas picked up his harp and began to play. Cathan wished she could stay and listen and forget about Erik, but how could she forget the way hunger had taken the laughter from his eyes? Trying to look as if she were just stepping outside for a moment, she rose to her feet and walked slowly to the door, nodding to the old grandmother, but once she was outside she broke into a run, heading straight across the moor grass. She was soon beyond the friendly sound of Seumas's music. Now all she could hear was the rustle of the wind in the dead bracken and the gurgling of the water in the burn as she made her way upstream. When she came to a sheep track that led down the steep bank, she crossed the water, jumping nimbly from one rock to the next, and then scrambled up the far side. By the time she reached Finger Rock the sun was setting and the sky was streaked with red. Erik wasn't there, but he had said after dark.

Cathan leaned back against the rock, her eyes following a flight of birds that seemed to pour down the smooth slope of the Cambir and out across the bay. As the birds approached the sky over Armunna's House, they suddenly took on the form of the tight crescent of the new moon. Something stirred in Cathan's mind. A memory, awakened from a distant time. This was the Sluagh, the Spirit Host. There would be a death in Gleann Mor before morning.

Cathan stood frozen against the rock, watching the last of the color fade from the sky. She wanted to go down to Gleann Mor to warn them about the Spirit Host, but no one could change what the spirits had set in motion. You could no more keep a soul from dying than the sun from setting. And it was as hard to keep a person whole in your mind once he was gone as to remember all the shades of color after the sun had set. Night overtook the island and Cathan stayed beside Finger Rock, waiting for Erik. The moon came up, a half moon with a ragged covering of wind-blown clouds rushing past it, and still Cathan waited. Though now she knew Erik wasn't going to come.

A sudden outburst of shouting from Armunna's

House jerked Cathan out of her trance. She began to run down the mountain in long, loping strides, even though it was so dark she couldn't see where to put her feet next. When she reached the rock fall, she had to slow down and she saw that the thatch on one of the cleits close to Armunna's House was burning. The night was filled with the sounds of screaming and shouting, while two small, dark figures fought against the bright backdrop of the fire. Then they moved and were lost in the smoke and darkness. Cathan forced herself to go faster, but fell and struck her knee against a sharp rock. She felt nothing. Her mind was ahead of her body, already down in Gleann Mor, and she began to cry, knowing what she would find. Erik had told her to go up to Finger Rock to keep her out of the way because he had known that the Vikings were going to come with spears against her people.

By the time Cathan reached Armunna's House the fighting was over. People were wandering about outside in a dazed, hopeless sort of way. Seumas's harp lay broken by the door. Seana, her face streaked with dirt and tears, was crouching over it.

"What happened, Seana? What has happened?" Cathan asked.

Seana was trying to put the pieces of the harp back together. She looked up at Cathan with flat, empty eyes.

"What happened?"

"Don't you know?" Seana asked. "They killed Seu-

mas . . . my Seumas . . . and Iain, too. The poor lads'
silly weapons were no match for Viking swords. And
they took away Liam and Marcus and Neill Rudh—
our best hunters. They tied them up with their own
ropes and they have dragged them off to Village Bay."

The old grandmother was outside, poking about in
the smoldering ashes of the burned-out fire. "First
they killed my Fergus," she lamented. "Fergus, who
knew more words than any of us, and now they've
destroyed the black book. Without the book that
contained all the wisdom of Brendan, what will become of us?"

Three other women were kneeling on the blood-
stained heather, wailing and keening for the dead.
Cathan joined them, with tears streaming down her
face, though she scarcely knew for whom she wept.
Iain and Seumas? Or Erik with the fine clothes and
golden hair? Erik, who had betrayed her after all.

11
A Test Of Courage

THE VIKING RAID led to a strange mixture of servitude
and freedom. Marcus, Liam, and Neill Rudh were
held as slaves in a house in Village Bay, roped together
day and night as if they were on the face of a cliff.
Their job was to provide food for their Viking masters
now that the birds were nesting all over the island.
They didn't mind scrambling about on the rocks of
Dun, collecting gulls' eggs and snaring guillemots, but
they did hate being penned up like sheep. The rest of
the islanders, on the other hand, now had more
freedom. The worst had happened, so they no longer
lived in fear. In spite of Seumas's and Iain's deaths, it
seemed that the Vikings had come to Gleann Mor that
night intending to take slaves and not to kill. If they
needed more slaves, they knew where to find them, so
there was no point in hiding. Donald Mac Ghillie even
recited the words from the black book: *As the Lord
forgives us, so also must we forgive them.*

But Cathan didn't listen. The black book had been destroyed in the fire. She wasn't going to forgive Erik. Not after the way he had betrayed her. He had told them who the best hunters were and where the food was stored. She sat by the fire, sad and silent. Her mother thought she grieved for Iain, which didn't make her load any lighter.

One morning Liam's little brother Tomas came stumbling into Armunna's House with the news that one of the Vikings had ordered Marcus and Liam to go down Conochair while he anchored the rope.

"Marcus and Liam would never go over the edge with a Viking holding the rope!" Roderick said.

"That's what Marcus was trying to tell them," Tomas explained.

"Aye, a man's life depends as much on his trust in his comrade as on the strength of the rope. How could anyone put his trust in a Viking?"

"Besides, it's too early in the season to be going down Conochair," Donald said. "The fulmars do not return to their nests if they are disturbed!"

However, curiosity about how it was going to turn out was so strong that they all set off for Conochair as if they'd been invited. Even Cathan went along. She hadn't seen Erik since the raid, but she noticed him right away, standing a little apart from the others. He looked well fed and his hair shone in the sun. She turned quickly away when he raised a hand, but he was only trying to get the attention of the Viking who was arguing with Marcus, Liam, and Neill Rudh. Then Erik walked over and spoke to Marcus. Marcus looked doubtful and shook his head. After a lot of pointing and hand waving, Liam picked up the rope.

"I think yon young Viking is offering to go down the cliff with one of our lads holding the rope," Cathan's mother said to Seana, edging closer.

" 'Twill even the score if young Liam lets the rope slip," Seana said bitterly.

"The Viking knows that," Roderick said with grudging respect. "He shows courage."

Marcus and Liam showed Erik how to tighten the snare on the end of the long fowling rod. The lad laughed at his own clumsiness when he couldn't flick the rod so that the noose of sinew would slip over a bird's head. After a few more lessons, Marcus seemed satisfied that Erik could use the rod and knotted a rope around his waist. Liam pointed out the best footholds.

Cathan could feel the tension in the crowd when Erik disappeared over the edge. They wanted him to succeed! Had they forgotten Iain and Seumas, and the way they had all been driven from their homes in Village Bay? They didn't even care that no one went down Conochair at nesting time. All for a small show of daring!

Cathan couldn't see the cliff face from where she

was standing. She could only watch Liam and Marcus directing Erik from above. He was gone for a very long time. At last his bright head reappeared, and when Liam pulled him to his feet, Cathan saw two fulmars swinging from his belt. A great cheer went up from the Hirtans as he showed them, without words, how he had snared the birds.

Skill on the cliffs ranked above all else on Hirta, so Erik's courage was like a soothing poultice. The islanders were suddenly eager to show the Vikings how to snare fulmars and drain the oil, though not everyone was as teachable as Erik. The old grandmother, noticing how worn Astrid looked, gave the young woman a jar of precious giben, made from the fat of young gannets or gugas. Although giben cured every ill, Cathan knew it wouldn't help Astrid, because it couldn't bring back the bairn that had died of want in the dark days.

By way of return, the Vikings gave the islanders milk from their cows and coarse hair from the manes of their ponies, which was soon in high demand for making snares and ropes.

Cautiously at first, and then more openly, the islanders began to move back into the houses around the village that remained empty. They didn't challenge the Vikings' right to the fields but planted their oats in Gleann Mor, as they had done the year before. And they still kept their sheep on the far side of the island.

But one problem hadn't been settled. The Vikings couldn't forget last winter's hunger. They wouldn't let their three slaves go. Liam and Marcus and Neill Rudh had to hand over every bird they caught to their masters, and they were not allowed to live with the other Hirtans. It troubled the islanders to see them walking glumly through the village trailing a rope. But no amount of talking could come up with a way to secure the slaves' freedom without upsetting the small freedoms they'd won for themselves.

"We must bide our time," Donald Mac Ghillie kept saying. "The way will surely present itself."

The men had gathered along the dyke to talk over plans for harvesting gugas from the ledges of Stac Armin, off Boreray.

"I think we should go tomorrow, if the weather remains fair," Roderick said.

Everyone had to give an opinion on the chances of a fine day, but before the matter was talked out, Erik came sauntering up from the field below the village. When it was clear that he meant to join the gathering, an awkward silence fell. Until now the Vikings had let the islanders settle their own affairs. However, as Erik drew closer, it was obvious that he was nervous, far more nervous than he'd been when he went down Conochair. He had something on his mind and didn't seem to know where to begin.

"What is it, then, lad?" Donald Mac Ghillie asked.

"I want the girl, Cathan, for a wife," Erik blurted out.

They didn't catch what he said the first time, so he had to say it again. His lack of language made the request sound abrupt, but when those nearest him caught the meaning, they quickly told the others and a slow smile spread through the crowd. The expedition to Stac Armin was forgotten. Before a man could marry, his future bride had to name the price. That this was the way to free Liam, Marcus, and Neill Rudh was so obvious that they didn't even need to talk about it. Alasdair went running off to fetch Cathan.

He found her working alongside the old grandmother, stacking peat.

When Cathan heard that she was wanted at the gathering right away, she was so surprised that she didn't even take the time to wash off the black mud that coated her arms to the elbows. Her hair was windblown and her face was red, but she flushed a deeper shade when she saw that Erik was among the men. She couldn't miss him, standing there half a head taller than the rest, his hair burnished by the bright sun.

"Before a lass leaps the Beltane fire with her man, it's our custom for the bride to ask him to do something for her first," Cathan's father was explaining to Erik.

Everyone turned toward Cathan, waiting for her to speak. She stared back at them. Had they all gone mad? How could her own father think of marrying her to one of the Viking kind after all that had happened? And then she realized what they wanted. She was to ask Erik to free Liam and Marcus and Neill Rudh. They were willing to give her in slavery to Erik, so that the men would be free.

"Name the price, Cathan," her father said.

Cathan's eyes hardened. She'd name the price! A girl had the right to ask a man to show his courage on the cliffs, in order to be sure she'd be well provided for.

"I'll have Erik balance on one heel at the edge of a rock," she said, "and place his other foot in front of the first, and then reach down and touch the foremost toe."

The men looked disappointed and began grumbling among themselves. Cathan was asking Erik to perform a child's trick. Alasdair jumped on the dyke to show Erik what he was to do.

Cathan raised her hand to get everyone's attention.

"He must do this up on the high arch on Ruaival . . . on the edge that hangs over the sea."

The grumbling stopped in a simultaneous intake of breath as the men pictured Erik. To stand on that wind-swept rock on one heel and lean forward with the sea as far below as the sky above—that would be a test worth watching!

"He cannot do it," someone whispered.

"When must the price be paid?" Cathan's father asked. He looked troubled because he liked the lad.

"Now," Cathan answered.

It was better to have it over with. She was already wishing she could take back the words.

Cathan's father and Erik led the way. Up past the church and the Tobar Well, then up the steep slope of Ruaival. Cathan followed with the men, and feeling their excitement—the same defiant eagerness that marked the first day of the fulmar hunt—she hated them for it. Someone was taking wagers on Erik's chances. When Roderick pointed out the dizzy height of the rock where Erik was to stand, Cathan caught his look of dismay, but she knew he wouldn't back out. She also knew that she was punishing herself as much as him.

Erik stopped at the place where the rocks rose in a steep stairway to the arch and took off his leather sandals, preferring to climb barefoot.

"It's our custom for the girl to wish her lad luck," Roderick said.

Erik scrambled up the stairway without waiting for Cathan's blessing. Perhaps he hadn't understood what Roderick said. Cathan herself was too afraid to speak as she watched him climb onto the flat stone that had fallen from the cliff to rest against another rock, forming an arch high above the churning sea. The very wind held its breath when the boy reached the farthest edge. Cathan closed her eyes, so she wasn't sure if the shouting and running feet and bouncing stones meant success or failure. Then Erik was back among them again, flushed and laughing. He had earned his place among the Hirtans. But Cathan saw that there was no love in his blue eyes when he finally looked her way.

She turned and ran. She kept to the high ground along the shoulder of Mullach Sgar and Mullach Bi, which took her past Finger Rock where she had waited that night when Erik didn't come. She looked along the smooth ridge of the Cambir and remembered the first time they met and how they had laughed together. She wanted to get away . . . far away. She crossed the glen and then toiled up the steep slope on the other side, not caring that it was growing dark.

The sun was coming up as Cathan stumbled to the top of Conochair. The first light of the new day colored the eastern sky. And the shadows of the standing stones lay long on the turf, twelve gray stones leaning into the wind.

"Caitlin! Caitlin!"

She turned around, hoping that Erik, tall and golden, had followed her up on the mountainside, but wasn't really surprised to see a slight, dark figure toiling up the slope toward her.

"Caitlin . . . Caitlin, I looked for you at the Beltane

fire . . . Where have you been? What are you doing up
here all by yourself?"

The plaintive sound in Dougal's voice was reassuring. And his words, too. She had come home, and no
one—except perhaps Feadair—knew she had been
gone. Cathan was somewhere in the time beyond . . .
and Erik, too.

12
QUEEN OF HIRTA

THE GIRLS, SITTING cross-legged in the long meadow grass, were making puffin snares from twisted strands of sinew. Una and Morda and Beitris were chattering and laughing together, but Caitlin hardly heard them. Almost two months had passed since the night of the Beltane fire, but the people from the other time were never out of her thoughts. Each morning her sense of loss at finding herself in the dark hut with the Old One was as sharp as it had been the first day. Sometimes she caught herself calling the old woman Grandmother or thinking of Sine's little ones as her own brothers and sisters. It was hard to share the excitement over who was going to catch the first puffin of the season and be named queen of Hirta with the memory of Erik's angry eyes nagging at her, but the sound of her name jerked her back to the present.

"Caitlin never talks to us these days—we're not good enough for her," Una was saying.

"She thinks she's already queen of Hirta!" Beitris teased, reaching for another strand of sinew.

Caitlin forced herself to join the laughter, but when Una began bragging about how many snares she was going to set on midsummer day, her thoughts drifted away again. By being in that other time she must have changed the time beyond that—but not in the way she would have chosen. She'd been more caught up in her own hurt feelings than in what was best for everybody. She'd thrown away the chance to ask for freedom for the slaves. And following her own feelings hadn't even resulted in what she wanted for herself. She hoped she hadn't lost Erik's love completely. Donald Mac Ghillie had been right when he recited those words from the black book about forgiveness. Keeping alive the wrongs of the past didn't put them right, and it was no way to bring peace to the island.

"Move over," Una said, nudging Caitlin back to the present once again. Una was spreading her snares out on the grass. "That makes three, with ten loops on each," she said, sounding pleased with herself.

Caitlin tied another loop to her snare, pulling the knot tight with her teeth, then carefully tested each loop till she was sure that the sinew slipped smoothly through the knots. She stuffed the snare into her pouch and jumped to her feet.

"Where are you going?" Morda asked, squinting up through her wind-tangled hair.

"To find out where the puffins are landing, so I'll know the best place to set my snare," Caitlin answered.

"You'll not catch many with only one snare," Beitris said.

"I need only catch one, if it's the first!"

The girls watched Caitlin with a mixture of envy and annoyance as she raced off through the buttercups and campion and then cut across the marshy ground near the Big Stream, jumping lightly from one hummock to the next. She was as flighty as a child, the way she never stuck to any task. Yet she had the independence of the Old One herself, heading off without a backward glance. And she wasn't even going up Ruaival, where the puffins nested in their burrows by the cliff's edge. Instead she was following the Big Stream up toward the pass to Gleann Mor. Not one of them would have dared go up there alone.

"She's looking for trouble," Una said uneasily. "One of these days she'll cross the path of a druid, and then what'll happen?"

"They say she's just like Morag, her mother," Morda said.

Caitlin suddenly disappeared from sight. But she hadn't been spirited away by the druids. She had dropped to her hands and knees and was creeping up over the top of the pass to the place where she could look down on Armunna's House through a screen of bracken. Armunna's House in Gleann Mor had been empty when the first lot of Vikings came, yet the druids had still been there—though not the white-cloaked druids that the islanders feared. They had been present in the Hirtans' grief over the felled oak trees. They were in Seumas's harp music and in her own song on the Cambir. She had felt them close beside her in the memory of the dark side when she was standing by Finger Rock and saw the shadow of the Spirit Host.

A group of druids emerged from Armunna's House, causing Caitlin's heart to beat a little faster, although they were so far away that they looked no bigger than white ants scurrying about in a meaningless pattern on the close-cropped turf. Then, in answer to some command that Caitlin couldn't hear, they came together and formed a long column that wound its way up Conochair. She watched until they were lost behind a shoulder of the hill, then followed them in her mind up to the circle of giant stones where they would wait for the sun to sink into the western sea. Soon it would be the shortest night of the summer. The islanders always stayed indoors that night, because they feared the dark side of the druid magic. But it was foolish to shut themselves away, afraid of the dark on the shortest night of the year. If the islanders and druids were going to be joined as one people, the way she'd seen it in that future time, they had to share their hunting skills and their knowledge . . .

And someone must take the first step.

It was always the men who harvested the fulmar chicks from the cliffs, but as far back as memory went, the first day of the puffin harvest belonged to the women. The girls left home at dawn to tend their snares, as nervous as nesting birds, each one of them dreaming of snaring the first puffin and being named queen of Hirta. It was hard to say why the honor meant so much. Perhaps it was the idea of being singled out from among the rest when everything else was shared. Besides, being chosen queen carried with it the promise of good luck, and no one turned her back on that.

"There's room on this rock over here, Caitlin," Una called, catching sight of Caitlin as she came bounding up the last stretch of Ruaival.

When Caitlin saw the number of snares Una had already stretched on the rock, she was immediately sorry she hadn't worked harder. What chance did she have of catching the first puffin with only one miserable snare? There was no use pretending she didn't care, but she wasn't going to make herself feel worse by sharing Una's rock.

"I'm putting mine here," she said, tossing her snare onto the nearest flat rock.

As soon as she had stretched out the snare and weighted it with stones, she could see that the place wasn't good. For one thing, it was too far from the edge of the cliff. But it was too late to join Una, because she was already crouching under her sheepskin cloak, so that if a puffin came close, all it would see would be a harmless ewe.

But a curious puffin had spotted the silvery gleam of Caitlin's snare and landed beside the sinew straggling across the stone. It tugged the sinew with its heavy red-tipped beak, gave a little hop, then tugged again. Caitlin saw the moment when the puffin felt the noose tighten around its orange webbed foot. The puffin struggled, flapping its wings, but it couldn't fly away.

"I've caught one! I've caught one!" Caitlin screamed, rushing to the snare and cupping her hands around the bird. Even in her excitement she managed to free its foot without breaking the snare.

Una and Morda and the other girls left their snares and came racing over to see the first-caught bird. They crowded close, waiting for a turn to hold it, bubbling with good-natured laughter. Caitlin was the only one who seemed surprised that her one snare—and poorly placed at that—had caught the first bird. Feeling the little creature trembling in her hands, she remembered from other years what happened next. She pulled a tuft of soft down from the breast, and the squawking bird was passed from hand to hand until it was plucked bare except for the wing and tail feathers. Then the bird was given back to Caitlin, who set it free on Una's rock. The naked bird flapped its wings and screamed with pain and anger, drawing other puffins in to see what was going on. Soon they too were trapped and became part of the noisy protest.

Now that the queen had been chosen, the girls settled to the task of catching birds, and the women joined them. Caitlin worked alongside the rest. Being queen didn't spare her from helping with the harvest. Her wool shift was soon sticking to her back and her hair was damp on her forehead as she rushed about tending the snares. After a while she joined the Old One, who was sitting next to a huge pile of birds with feathers flying around her head like a snow flurry in winter. Caitlin worked steadily beside the old woman, plucking the birds until her fingers were numb and her teeth ached from pulling out the stout wing and tail feathers. The little naked carcasses were split and hung up to dry. The Old One couldn't pull the wing feathers with her toothless gums, but her twisted fingers plucked the down as quick as any. Suddenly she turned to Caitlin, her black eyes twinkling wickedly, and said, "I suppose with luck running on your side today, you'll be after Rona's lad Dougal! Your mother Morag put her spell on Tormod Rudh the day she was chosen queen, and he never came out of it."

"I wouldn't go wasting my luck on the likes of Dougal," Caitlin snapped.

" 'Twould be foolish indeed to waste today's luck, lass, but it would be more foolish to go after something you cannot see an end to." The Old One paused for a moment, then continued seriously, "A bairn brought into the world on the night of a storm often seeks out danger, and that is how it has been with you, Caitlin. The way you would not stay away from the cliffs and rocks when you were small. Aye, and the way you wander off by yourself now that you are nearly grown, deliberately choosing places where the druids go. Have you no fear of the dark magic? Don't go thinking that a little bit of luck is any match for that."

It was then, in the face of the Old One's warning, that Caitlin knew what she was going to do. Today, while she was queen of Hirta and luck was on her side, she would go to the druids and take the first step in bringing understanding between her people and theirs.

13
THE DRUID CIRCLE

ALTHOUGH IT WAS still light, the islanders had already fallen into bed to dream of flying feathers and puffin meat. All except Caitlin. She was climbing Conochair. Looking back, she saw the whole valley deep in the shadow of Ruaival. She would have to hurry if she was going to reach the circle of stones before the sun went down.

When the stones were finally visible against the sky, Caitlin felt the same rush of relief as when she dragged herself up onto a cliff top after a hard climb. The druids were there, just as she'd known they would be. And it was as if they had known she would come, because a tall woman with hair as yellow as the marsh marigolds growing by the Big Stream came forward to meet her. Caitlin was surprised at seeing the woman— only men blessed the well and came to the Samain fire—and she looked around anxiously, hoping to find Feadair. The druids all looked the same in their white cloaks, though some were young, as young as she was. She had to find Feadair soon because the flaming sun was already flattening itself against the sea. The woman with the yellow hair, apparently guessing that Caitlin was about to speak, raised her finger to her lips. Then she wrapped a soft white cloak around Caitlin's shoulders, fastened it with a clip of carved oak, and placed a garland of oak leaves on her head.

As the sun disappeared, Caitlin felt a rush of fear, but the druids began to move with slow, shuffling steps and she was carried along with them as they encircled the stones, walking deasil, the way of the sun, the way of the seasons, the way of the druids. The girl's feet moved of their own volition. It was as if she had again stepped into another life and had become one with all the others walking there. Cloaked figures, hooded figures, silent shadows in the whispering dark. On midsummer night there was scarcely an hour of darkness from sunset to sunrise, yet Caitlin felt as if she had been walking with the druids since the beginning of time.

Suddenly a voice rang out, the Stallir's voice, commanding them to stop and turn east to greet the rising sun as it came out of the sea. The Fire that Water could not drown. Feadair was playing his harp, but the strains of the music were lost in the screaming cries of a thousand birds waking to the frenzy of a new day. The air was filled with swooping birds, like spindrift in a storm. Watching them in their glorious freedom, Caitlin experienced a new awareness and saw herself as if from high above—the robe of soft white wool, the garland of leaves on her head, her hair, burnished red by the rising sun, loose about her shoulders and blowing in the wind. Without having to be told, she turned to face back into the circle at the moment the sun rose out of the sea. She could see everyone clearly now, twenty, thirty, or more, men and women, boys and girls, all dressed in long white robes, forming a circle around the granite stones.

The slanting rays of the newly risen sun cast long shadows, and Caitlin felt a moment of panic when she saw that her shadow lay across the fallen stone. The turf had been cleared away from around its edge, so it was raised a little, like a low table. Feadair, staring at the shadow, seemed at that instant to grow old and colorless. His long fingers stopped plucking the harp and even the bird cries were stilled. Yet the silence screamed as loud as storm winds in winter.

Beyond Feadair, the Stallir was staring down at the shadow, the dark side of the druid magic in his cruel, granite gaze. Caitlin's heart began to pound. With fumbling fingers, she undid the clip that held her cloak and shrugged free of it, letting it fall to the ground like the husk of a dragonfly's skin when it emerges from the muddy depth of a pond. She began to run, not thinking which way she went, only wanting to escape. The garland of oak leaves slipped from her hair. A little of yesterday's luck still held, because the stones were so near the cliff's edge that she could have easily fallen to her death, but instead Caitlin's panicked flight took her straight down into Gleann Mor and then up on the Cambir, where a cold, wet mist had rolled in from the sea, blotting out everything, both sun and shadow. She gave a moan of terror when the mist in front of her grew thicker and congealed into the shape of a man, a white-cloaked druid. For a terrible moment she thought it was the Stallir. But the angry voice calling her by name belonged to Feadair. Looking up at him, she saw that the anger didn't match the pain in his eyes.

"What brought you there? What did you hope for, joining the druid circle and throwing yourself in the Stallir's path?"

Caitlin hung her head. How could she—a skinny girl with arms mottled blue from the cold and hair as lank as seaweed—tell him that she'd come as queen of Hirta to share their ceremony in friendship instead of fear? She'd gone so long without sleep that her brain was fuddled and she couldn't find the right words.

"Do you know nothing of the dark side?" The druid's voice was hard.

"I thought it only existed in our own fear," Caitlin whispered.

"How could you be so foolish?" Feadair asked. "There can be no light without the dark, any more than there can be day without the night. Without the threat of the dark magic, the villagers have no reason to give us a share of the food at Samain. Without the fear of the spirits of the afterworld, they would have driven us from Hirta long ago . . . as some of them are scheming to do even now."

"So it's fear on both sides that keeps us apart," Caitlin said, surprised by the idea that the druids might be afraid too. Afraid because they depended on the islanders for food.

"And you thought you could do away with fear! But instead you have forced the Stallir to call down the dark magic to restore the balance of fear, and that will drive our peoples further apart. There will be no living together as one people now . . . and in the ensuing violence, the stories will all be lost, the songs will be still . . . and the only voices left on Hirta will belong to the screaming sea birds and the crying wind."

But Caitlin couldn't think beyond herself. "What is the Stallir going to do?" she asked.

The answer—too terrible for words—came directly into her mind. The shadow that darkened the stone in summer foretold whose blood would stain the sacrifice stone in winter. In years when hunger gnawed and storms gripped the island past the time when the birds should return, the Stallir brought back the light by appeasing the dark.

The color drained from Caitlin's face, and her eyes were wide with fear.

"Perhaps it need never happen," Feadair said gently. "I think I can save you from the Stallir's dark magic, child. Aye, even at the price of changing everything that is yet to be."

"Why . . . why would you do that?" Caitlin asked.

"Surely you know!" Feadair answered. "Didn't you guess the meaning of the token Morag gave you, child?" His voice was as low and gentle as if he were crooning a love song to the music of his harp. "I am your father, Caitlin. When your mother left you the token, that is what she was telling you."

Caitlin backed away from Feadair. "Tormod Rudh was my father!"

"Nay, child! You belong to me."

"It isn't true!" Caitlin shouted angrily. "Tormod Rudh is my father. I won't listen to you! I won't let you take my father away from me!"

"You are one of us, Caitlin. How else do you think you came by the power to travel to the time beyond?"

"I don't believe you!" Caitlin shouted.

Feadair's words were as frightening as the Stallir's dark magic because they could destroy her memories of Tormod Rudh. By telling her that Tormod Rudh was not her father, Feadair was killing him again, giving him a second death. She was not going to let that happen. Not to Tormod Rudh who had gone looking for a ewe that had lambed early on the day of her birth . . . Tormod Rudh who had taught her to live fearlessly. She turned and ran blindly into the mist.

14
BAINE

THE BOY SEEMED to draw his shape out of the thinning mist. A small boy, eight or nine years old, with loose leather britches and a thick scarf crossed over his chest. His skinny red legs and wrists stuck out like twigs from the bulkiness of his clothes, but his most noticeable feature was his hair, which was as white as a gull's breast.

"Catie! Catie! Caaaa-tie, where are you? I know you're there!"

Catie . . . Catie . . . the name and the high, musical sound of the voice spread into the spaces in Caitlin's mind, wiping out every thought except that she'd been looking for this boy for a long time. Her relief at finding him safe turned to annoyance the moment she saw him. She ducked behind a boulder, thinking she'd keep out of his way a bit longer to punish him for running away and frightening her. A branch of heather snapped under her foot and the boy spun around.

"You *are* there, Catie! I know it's you."

Catie stepped back into the open, but the boy didn't look at her. He stood very still, with his head tilted.

"You scared me, running off like that," Catie said.

The boy smiled, but Catie could see tears hanging from his thick white lashes as they fluttered against his cheeks. So he'd been scared, too, though he'd never admit it.

"I can find my way over the whole island!"

"There's the cliffs, Baine," Catie answered, the boy's name coming as easily as her own acceptance of the name Catie.

"The birds let me know when I'm near the edge—and the wind."

"What about when the mist comes up?" Catie asked severely. "The mists change sound and can trick a blind person as sure as people who see. Come on home, Baine. Your mam'll be worrying."

Baine rested his hand lightly on Catie's arm as she chose the way for both of them. It was easy walking over the short, tough grass on the Cambir, but even when they were climbing up to the pass, Baine seemed able to anticipate every rock and cleit. Both Catie and Baine were eight years old, and were the same height, but Catie looked sturdier in her blue wool dress that flapped about her ankles. Her dark hair seemed almost black beside Baine's white head.

"Tell me everything you can see," Baine said when

the wind gusted against their faces at the top of the pass. "Then I'll make you a song."

This was a game they often played together.

"The mist has gone and the sky is all-over blue," Catie said. She tipped back her head to take in the bigness of it. "Swept clean by the wind, though there's still a wisp wrapped around Conochair, like Mam's shawl. The birds are dancing, riding the wind. The sea is all-over blue, too, but stirred up where the waves are spitting on the rocks."

"Are the men still talking along the dyke?"

"No . . . no, they're not."

"Where are they, then? What are they doing?" Baine asked impatiently, hearing the puzzlement in Catie's voice.

"They're down at the beach. Everyone is. There's a boat, Baine! A boat way out in the bay."

"What kind of boat? Can it be the steward?"

"It's not the right time," Catie answered.

The steward came over from the Hebrides each August after the fulmars had been harvested to collect the rent for the laird—bales of wool and feathers and mutton and fulmar meat. In exchange he brought the islanders salt and sugar from the mainland, and sometimes things they couldn't find a use for. Catie and Baine always looked forward to the steward's coming.

"You go on home, Baine, and I'll find out what's happening," Catie said when they reached the dyke.

She didn't listen to the little boy's angry protest, but went flying off down the track to the beach and reached the rock jetty in time to see a sailor in the prow of the boat hurl a coil of rope to Angus MacQueen on the shore.

"Easy, now! Easy!" Angus shouted as a wave drove the boat toward the rocks.

Catie wriggled between Niall Fergusson and Dubh Finlay to get a better look. The steward was in the boat right enough, but he was making no move to come ashore. Two men were unloading a big black wooden chest. This was followed by a woman, who was dumped onto the jetty with no more ceremony than landing a struggling sheep from Soay. The islanders watched silently as the woman scrambled to her feet and shook her fist at the men in the boat, accompanying the gesture with a stream of meaningless words. This was the first woman Catie had ever seen from the mainland, and she couldn't take her eyes off the woman's clothes. Her coat, which was the color of bell heather in summer, was fitted to her waist and fastened with real buttons. Under it she wore a dress like sunshine, with flowers growing around the hem. Her wild hair and face didn't match her splendid clothes. Her complexion was dark and pockmarked, and a jagged scar cut across her right cheek from below her eye to the corner of her mouth.

When the woman realized that the boat was casting off, a whining note crept into her voice. She reached into her pocket and brought out a piece of silver, holding it up so that the men on the boat could see it.

"Keep your money, Lady Grange," one of them shouted, pulling at his oar. "You'll need it for buying things in all the fine shops on Hirta!"

The rest of the sailors thought this a huge joke. The boat slipped away to the sound of their laughter, leaving the bewildered islanders with the strange woman in their midst. Although she didn't speak a word of their tongue, she immediately made it plain that she didn't want to be there.

"The steward will be back," Angus MacQueen told everyone.

"Not before summer . . ."

"We'll have to find her somewhere to stay."

"There's the house over by the main dyke," Niall Fergusson suggested.

The cottage that Niall pointed out was nearer the shore than the rest of the village and had stood empty since the sickness of 1727 claimed so many lives. When the matter was finally considered settled, Angus Mac-Queen bade his wife Morag to bring the box.

The wooden chest was too heavy for Morag to lift, so Catie's mother helped her. They carried it along the jetty and over the rocks to the beach, with the stranger lurching and slipping behind them. She scrabbled over the seaweed on all fours like a bairn not yet able to walk, her beautiful red coat dragging in a tide pool. The rest of the islanders followed along behind her, keeping their distance, but still close enough to watch her every move. Morag shouted to her daughter Anna to run home and fetch a blanket and dry bracken for the crub.

"And an oil lamp," Catie's mother called after Anna. "The poor woman'll need a light."

The house had no windows or chimney, but that made it all the more snug when the wind was blowing. Catie watched until the woman had gone inside. Then she raced off to tell Baine all about the stranger. She could see him still sitting on the dyke. Sulking because she'd left him, she guessed.

"There was a woman in the boat, Baine," Catie shouted as soon as she was close enough to be heard. "A woman from the mainland."

"You said I might fall over the cliffs . . ." Baine said.

"Not here in Village Bay," Catie interrupted impatiently. "Do listen! The steward's boat brought a woman. Lady Grange, they called her—and they've left her here. Her clothes are lovely, Baine. She's got flowers on her dress like none I've ever seen on Hirta."

"Where is she now?" Baine asked, sliding down from the dyke. "Take me to her."

"I wouldn't dare, Baine! She acts half-crazed!"

For the rest of the afternoon and into the evening the younger children, Catie and Baine among them, kept a close watch on Lady Grange's house. Some of the children said she was a witch and that her strange words were spells, but others argued that that was just how the people from the mainland spoke. Although they were all curious to have another look at her, when she finally came to the door and peered out, the children dashed for home, skirting around the corner of the bottom field. Catie and Baine were the last to leave, and cut through the long grass to catch up with the rest.

"Look at Catie!" wee Seumas shouted. "She and Baine are walking on Fergus's Place!"

"We're not hurting anything—it's only grass," Catie shouted back, though she knew as well as any of them that it was bad luck to step on Fergus's Place, even though no one knew why or who Fergus was.

"The witch'll put a spell on you!" Mary Finlay chanted.

"She's not a witch," Catie declared, but she did wish she'd paid more attention to where she was leading Baine. To get away from Mary's teasing, she and Baine ducked into the MacQueens' cottage, the first house they came to.

Mrs. MacQueen was dishing up a bowl of fulmar meat.

"Take this bite of supper down to that poor woman, Anna," she told her daughter.

"Can I just leave it outside her door?" Anna asked.

"You'll have to take it in—or how is she going to know it's there?"

"I don't want to go inside," Anna said. "Why did the steward bring her here? And why do we have to look after her?"

"It is our way to take in the stranger who comes to these shores, Anna. Who can tell—we may be entertaining an angel unawares."

"That was no angel talking to those sailors on the boat," Anna answered, giggling.

Catie thought Anna was the prettiest girl on Hirta. Her hair was more gold than red, and her skin was fair. She was nearly six years older than Catie and Baine. In spite of that, she often played with them—though this last year she seemed to prefer Dubh Finlay's company to theirs.

"I'll take the bowl," Catie offered, wanting to please Anna.

"Well . . . I suppose you could, Catie," Mrs. Mac-Queen said a little doubtfully. "Don't go slopping it over."

"I'll be careful," Catie promised.

Baine, her constant shadow, followed Catie from the house. The sky over Ruaival was now streaked with clouds, deep red in the setting sun. The birds, catching the sun's last rays, were turned from white to gold.

"Red sky at night, sailor's delight," Catie chanted, spilling some of the stew because she was looking at the sky instead of at her feet.

"Is it a pretty sunset?" Baine asked wistfully.

"It is that," Catie answered. "The sky is deep red, like Lady Grange's coat, and the birds are as gold as her dress."

When they reached the house near the main dyke, Catie remembered Anna asking her mam if she could just leave the bowl outside. Now Catie didn't like the idea of going in either. Maybe the strange woman was a witch after all.

"If we just set it down and shouted . . ."

"I want to see her," Baine said.

"You can't, Baine!" Catie answered sharply. "Seeing" meant touching, and Catie wasn't going to let Baine get that close to a woman who might be a witch. But Baine didn't listen. He began feeling his way along the stone wall and gave a little grunt of satisfaction when he found the door. He pushed against it and it swung open. They both froze at the harsh sound of the woman's voice.

"Who's she talking to?" Baine whispered.

"Hush!" Catie said.

The words, if they were words, made no sense, yet they had a rhythm to them as if they might mean something after all. Catie followed Baine inside, sniffing the dank air. No one had kindled the fire, but at least the fulmar oil lamp was burning. The woman was crouching over her wooden box, apparently reading by the flickering light. Catie's hands began to shake so much she could scarcely hold the bowl. The woman was a witch right enough, reading spells from a big black book. There was nowhere to put the bowl except on the box right next to the woman. Catie knew her legs wouldn't take her that far, but Baine was walking steadily toward the voice.

Lady Grange's words broke off and she swung around. With the light at her back, Catie couldn't see her face, but when Baine stumbled against the woman, she held out her arms and caught him. He fitted himself against her, rubbing his cheek on her soft coat and touching her skirt lightly with his fingers.

"I've—I've brought your supper," Catie stammered.

Lady Grange reached past Baine and grabbed the bowl. She dipped her fingers into the broth and fished out a piece of fulmar, stuffing it hungrily into her mouth. The next moment she spat the meat onto the floor and began to rage at Catie. Catie grabbed Baine and pulled him out of the house.

"I—I don't know what made her so angry," Catie said as she led Baine around Fergus's Place. She wasn't taking any more chances today. "She didn't seem to like the meat, Baine. Do you suppose they don't like fulmar on the mainland?"

But Baine wasn't interested. "Now I know what red is like," he said, smiling happily. "It's rough—but soft and warm under your fingers. And yellow is slippery as a fish, but not so wet and cold."

"What are you going on about?" Catie asked.

"Colors! I saw red and yellow in there . . . show me more colors, Catie."

In the short time they'd been inside Lady Grange's house, the sun had disappeared. The sky was still tinged with red, but the land was shadowed in blue and black. It was all too hard to put into words.

"It's nighttime now," Catie said. "The colors have all gone, Baine."

They were passing old Nan Finlay's house and the sweet smell of hay and warm milk and manure wrapped around them. Nan was singing against the soft lowing of her cow. She often sat in the byre singing after the milking was done. Her little heifer would look black in the darkness of the byre, but it occurred to Catie that by running your hand over its rough coat, you'd know it was brown in your mind, as if it were still daylight.

"Come here, Baine! I'll show you brown!" she said.

Old Nan stopped singing at the sight of the children in the doorway. "You've come at the right time to take the cow to the bottom field, lass," she said. "It'll save my old legs. I was sitting here awhile, hoping you'd drop by."

"I'll take it if you'll give us a taste of milk," Catie bargained. Nan nearly always gave them milk warm from the cow, and Catie was thinking that after all those errands the pot might be empty by the time she reached home.

Nan let them drink from the dipper. Catie wiped the white foam from around her mouth with the back of her hand, and Baine licked his mouth clean with his

tongue. Then the old woman gave the lead rope to
Catie. She led the cow out of the byre, with Baine one
step behind her, resting his hand on the cow's flank.
Catie picked her way hesitantly down the dark track,
while Baine walked with the same concentrated care-
fulness as always. And while they walked, he sang.
Some of the words were from Nan Finlay's song, but
the tune came by itself. Baine had a gift for music. His
mam said he got it from the wee folk, for he'd once
wandered off when he was little and had been gone for
three days and three nights. It was Catie who had
found him and brought him back. As his song rose in
the darkness, Catie thought that it was easy to believe
his singing was a gift from the wee folk.

"A brown cow, a brown cow, a brown cow
   for Catie,
A brown cow, a brown cow, that would
   milk the milk for thee,
Ho ro ru ra ree, a cow in the fold,
Ho ro ho ro ru ra ree."

15
THE STEWARD'S VISIT

THE SUMMER SEASON followed its well-ordered rhythm
of labor and song and honoring the Maker. Digging
the peat and planting the oats. The blessing of the
Tobar Well and then the puffin hunt, with Anna
catching the first bird and being named queen of
Hirta. The midsummer ceremony at Armunna's
House in Gleann Mor and the gannet expedition to
Boreray. And through it all, the presence of the
stranger was like a dark thread. The villagers left food
for her each day, and oil for her lamp. They stacked
peat by her door and brought water from the well.
Angus MacQueen wove her a new blanket. But Lady
Grange didn't respond to their kindness. She was still
so full of rage that when she met any of them, it spilled
over in a torrent of meaningless words.

Along the head dyke the men had talked about the
stranger long after they had anything left to say. From
her way of talking, they guessed she was from the

mainland and not from the Hebrides. The steward had told them about the mainland, where you couldn't see the land for trees and where there were more kinds of food than anyone on Hirta could imagine. Perhaps those strange foods hadn't agreed with Lady Grange. Niall Fergusson said she acted as if she suffered from colic, but Dubh Finlay was quick to point out that she wasn't improving on a wholesome diet of fulmar and oatmeal. Finally they returned to the old stories. Iain Gillies began telling about the time before his father was born, when the men had gone over to Boreray and a storm had come up. The wind didn't stop blowing for seven long months, and the men had stayed on Boreray all winter.

"The women went up to the Gap on Conochair each morning to look for a message from Boreray. The hillside was always green, and the women gave thanks. But when the men came back in the spring, they'd been gone so long that their own wives didn't know them!"

Everyone laughed.

"Have you heard that Alisdair has a new way of catching guillemots?" young Dubh Finlay asked.

"Yesterday evening Dubh and I caught a hundred birds in less than an hour," Alisdair boasted. "We drove the birds from their perches on Ruaival, and then Dubh lowered me to a ledge with a piece of white cloth over my head."

"The birds thought he was a rock covered with bird droppings when they came flying back to roost—"

"And then it was just a matter of picking them out of the air!" Alisdair broke in, reaching out to show the men how he'd done it.

The talk moved on to the fulmar harvest and the coming of the steward, and that brought them back to the stranger. Surely the steward would take her away to the mainland when he came this year.

Shortly before the fulmar harvest, the women brought the cattle and ewes back to Village Bay, so as not to spend as long over the milking, and the men drew lots to see which part of the cliff would be theirs. Although each man worked his own section, the entire catch was piled on the cliff top and then divided, each family receiving a share. The only birds a hunter ever kept for himself were those found away from the nest, for they would be lost to the ravens and hawks anyway.

On the long-awaited morning the children followed the women up Conochair, where the first catch of fulmar was ready to be plucked. Even early in the day the sun was hot, and Catie soon shed her thick blue dress and wore only a short wool shift like most of the other girls. Her job was to collect the oil, then hand the bird to Baine to pluck. She squeezed the bird gently so that the rust-red oil flowed from its bill into a bag made from a gannet's stomach. It was dirty work, and Catie was soon covered with oil and feathers, but she loved the singing and the old tales that were as much a part of the harvest as the flying feathers. Nan Finlay had come over to sit among the children and they were begging her for a story.

"Tell us about the first steward," little Mary Finlay said.

"About Coll MacLeod!" Baine chimed in.

"Aye, tell us a story!" wee Seumas said, tossing a handful of feathers into the air.

Nan waited quietly until they were busy again. "Long, long ago, the MacLeods of Harris and the MacDonalds of Uist both laid claim to the islands that lay on the edge of the world," she began. "To decide the matter once and for all, they agreed to a race. The first man to touch land would win the islands for his clan and chief. It was a fair race, with the boats alike and an equal number of oars in each. And it turned out to be a close race, with scarce a boat's length between them all the way. Then, when they had almost reached the cliffs of Oiseval, the MacDonalds pulled ahead. Their victory yell drowned out the screaming cries of the sea birds, and the MacLeods slumped over their oars, for they could see defeat. But young Coll MacLeod—"

"Was not a man who let himself be beaten," Baine interrupted, unable to keep quiet, for this was the best part of the story.

"Aye, Coll MacLeod, in the stern of the losing boat, was not a lad to accept defeat," Nan continued. "He clambered forward to the prow, drawing his sword. With a shout of triumph, he severed his left hand and sent it flying over the heads of the MacDonalds, painting a great rainbow of blood in the sky. No one could say that a MacLeod was not the first to touch the land, and so MacLeod of MacLeod has been lord of these islands from that day to this. Each year he sends his steward to collect the rent of feathers and fulmar oil, and he brings us salt for preserving our meat and sometimes a piece of fine red cloth or a bag or two of oats for next year's planting."

"Do you think that this year he'll take the stranger back?" Catie asked.

"Maybe as part of the rent!" Mary suggested.

The steward's visit was overdue and the islanders could talk of nothing else. A lookout had been posted on Oiseval to watch for the boat. Lady Grange seemed to know that it was time for him to come and waited with as much eagerness as the rest. But the two people who were most impatient of all were Dubh Finlay and Anna MacQueen, because when the steward came, they were going to be wed. The marriage feast of bannock cakes and eggs and mutton and cheese was ready.

But first Dubh had to prove himself worthy of his lass.

The day after the boat finally arrived, Dubh was taken up Ruaival to stand on the Mistress Stone. Everyone on the island came to watch. Baine walked alongside Catie, his hand resting on hers, sensing the rocks and the rough places on the ground.

When Catie saw the arched rock of the Mistress Stone ahead of them she felt a strange chill run through her. Dubh Finlay was already climbing up to it and a hush had fallen over the watching crowd.

"What's happening?" Baine whispered. "Tell me about it."

But Catie had closed her eyes. Even so, she could see the lad standing on the lip of the rock, balancing on the heel of his left foot. A tall, golden boy—though Dubh was dark.

"He's going to put his right foot in front of his left, then lean over and hold on to his toe," Catie explained to Baine. "He's standing on the edge of the Mistress Stone over the sea."

"Does every man have to stand up there before he can marry?" Baine asked.

"Aye! He must prove his courage on the cliffs—how else could he support a wife?" Catie answered. "It has always been that way."

She opened her eyes and saw Anna standing with her head thrown back, smiling proudly up at her lad, without a trace of fear. Catie's own heart was hammering as if it were going to burst.

The steward stayed with the MacQueens, and the rest of his men were distributed among the other families in the village. The men made outrageous demands—like wanting bannocks and mutton and cheese at every meal instead of boiled fulmar or guillemot. All the same, the villagers enjoyed their guests, with their tales of that strange place they called Outside. This year the story everyone wanted to hear, before they even got around to discussing the rent, was why the strange woman had been brought to Hirta.

The men, seated along the dyke, heard the story first from the steward himself.

"Her husband, Lord Grange, is a judge of the Court of Session in Edinburgh," the steward explained. Nobody knew what that meant, but they listened politely as he continued. "They lived in a fine house in Niddry's Wynd, just off the High Street. Edinburgh is a grand city, with as many houses as there are sheep on Hirta, a church with a steeple as high as yonder cliffs, and a castle built on a rock."

"Aye, it must be a grand place," Angus MacQueen agreed, nodding wisely, although all the sheep turned into houses made a confusing picture in his mind.

"Lord Grange and his wife didn't get along, and finally he turned her out of the house. To get even with him, she stood out in the street under his window, waving papers that she claimed proved he'd been on the side of the Jacobites back in the 1715 Rebellion."

"That would be one of the wars," Niall Fergusson said.

Each year, when the steward came, the islanders asked about the latest war. There was always a war somewhere. They thought it strange the way the people Outside, who already had so much, always seemed to need a bit more and fought wars to get it.

"If people heard that Lord Grange had been disloyal to the king, he'd lose his position as judge," the steward went on. "He was worried they'd listen to his wife's raving, so he had Lord Lovat and his men take her over to Heskeir in the Hebrides, where it wouldn't matter much what she said. They're a barbarous lot, these Lovats. They weren't too gentle with Lady Grange, as you can see from the scar on the poor woman's face. Then, when she tried to bribe her way off Heskeir, they told me to bring her here, knowing that escape from Hirta is well-nigh impossible."

"So you'll not be taking her back?" Angus asked.

"It would be more than my life is worth," the steward answered. "I can't go against Lord Lovat and the judge of the Court of Session in Edinburgh. The poor woman'll just have to make the best of it here."

16
LADY GRANGE

THE ISLANDERS FOUND it hard to understand the stranger's long despair when the steward left without her. She had stout walls against the weather and was well fed. And they went on feeding her without even a nod of thanks. Were their own lives not shaped by happenings over which they had no control? The wind and the weather, the return of the birds in the spring, the ripening of the oats, even the pieces of driftwood washed into the bay. As the months went by they paid the stranger less and less heed. She became just another chore for the young ones, who took turns at leaving a bowl of food and a bucket of water at her door each day. The older girls replenished the peat stack when it was low.

One evening, when Catie and Baine were setting a bowl of oatmeal and fresh sorrel by the door, one of the dogs came sniffing around the corner.

"We'd better take her supper inside," Catie said. "If we don't, Brac's going to get to it first."

She pushed the door open but stopped abruptly when she heard a low, wailing sound.

"She's crying," Baine whispered.

It was strange to hear a grown woman cry like a bairn in the night.

"What'll we do?" Catie asked.

They hovered near the open door until Baine finally led the way in. Once Catie's eyes had adjusted to the darkness, she saw that the fire in the middle of the floor wasn't completely dead. Squatting down, she blew until the peat glowed. Then she lit the lamp. By this time the woman had stopped crying and was sitting on her box with Baine pulled close to her. She had on a black dress and a gray woolen shawl wrapped around her shoulders. She began to croon softly, all the while stroking Baine's white head. Catie couldn't make sense of the song at all, but Baine joined in, copying the words. Now that the woman was calm, Catie wanted to leave, but she couldn't abandon Baine. She sat there for an hour, listening to the woman sing and babble.

"Why couldn't you have tried to get away sooner?" Catie asked Baine as soon as they were outside again.

"She thought I was one of her bairns," he said. "She misses them."

"The steward never said a thing about bairns," Catie snapped. "You can't know that!"

"I can so," Baine maintained. "I know what she's saying—not everything. But I could tell she thought her child had come back. And she wants us to help her get away."

"Don't be daft, Baine! Even the steward couldn't help her. Do you want Lord Lovat after you? And the judge? There's not a thing we can do."

That winter, Baine took to spending long hours in Lady Grange's house. He went alone. Catie told herself she didn't care, but she sorely missed his company and his songs. Even when he did come to her house, he didn't seek her out the way he used to do. Then one day, just before the puffins came back, he appeared at Catie's door, saying that he needed her help. Hiding her eagerness, Catie grabbed her sheepskin cloak.

"You're to come to Lady Grange's house," Baine said.

"You know the way there on your own," Catie answered sharply. "You go there often enough!"

"There's something she wants you to do . . ." The rest of Baine's words were lost as they stepped out into the wind.

Lady Grange was reading strange words from her black book and didn't look up when they walked in. Baine, who must have heard the words before, began to say them along with her:

"Cast thy bread upon the waters: for thou shalt find it after many days. Give a portion to seven and also to eight; for thou knowest not what evil shall be on the earth."

Lady Grange slammed the book shut.

"That's what we're going to do!" she said, looking straight at Catie with wild black eyes. "We'll cast my message on the waters!"

Catie edged closer and watched, round-eyed, when the woman picked up a quill and made marks on a piece of paper, writing the way the steward did. Fancy a woman being able to write as well as read! She took a step backward when the woman waved the paper in her face.

"She wants you to take it and throw it into the sea, so that the waves will carry the words to her friends," Baine told Catie. "When they know where she is, they'll come in a boat to rescue her."

"How do you know that's what she wants?" Catie asked.

"That's what she was telling us," Baine said.

Catie took the flimsy paper from the woman's hand. It was strange to think that a person's thoughts and wishes could be trapped on paper and held there. But even if Catie wasn't clever enough to read and write, she did know that it would be foolish to throw the message into the sea in the bay. The waves would bring it right back to shore. But if she climbed far enough out along the rocks on Oiseval, the paper might be carried around the headland to the open sea. She'd seen the way the men had to pull on the oars to get the boat out into the bay, but then the current carried them past Oiseval. And after that, there was nothing between Hirta and the Hebrides.

With the paper clutched tightly in Catie's hand, the children crossed the fields and the dry burn. Now and then Catie glanced back at the village and was glad to see that nobody was about. Mam wouldn't like her taking Baine along the steep shoulder of Oiseval above the water. The sheep trail they followed took them higher than Catie wanted to be, so they had to angle down the slick grassy slope. Baine followed confidently, but when the grass gave way to mud and rock just above Coll Point, Catie stopped.

"You'll have to wait here, Baine," she said.

Baine scowled, the way he always did when he was told there were places he couldn't go, but he didn't try to follow.

Down on the wave-washed rocks along the shore, Catie paused to gather a few whelks and poke a red sea anemone in a tide pool. She should have helped Baine down the cliff side after all. He'd have liked to feel an anemone wrap its tentacles around his finger. Several small crabs scuttled for cover in the sea-wrack as she hoisted herself onto a boulder. When she was as close to the waves as she dared go, she tossed the message into the water. But at that moment, the wind gusted, catching the paper and sending it fluttering up over her head into a crevice on the cliff behind her. She dragged herself to where she thought she'd seen it land but found only a white stain of bird droppings. The paper, with Lady Grange's words, had disappeared.

As Catie scrambled back up to Baine, it crossed her mind that she could easily tell him that the paper had floated off like a feather in the wind, and then been carried on the waves around the headland. He wouldn't know the difference. But she never lied to him.

And so she told him that the paper hadn't gone anywhere.

"It went somewhere," he pointed out.

"It blew up on the rocks. Nobody's going to find it there, except the birds."

They retraced their steps along the side of the hill and then trailed along the beach. Catie picked up a small piece of wood that had caught in the seaweed at the high tide mark. It nestled comfortably in her hand, almost like a little bird.

"What we need to do is tie the paper to something heavy, so I could throw it farther," she said, swinging the wood in her hand. "Something that would float like a piece of driftwood."

Baine explained the idea to Lady Grange, and soon Catie wished she'd never thought of it. The strange woman took to roaming the beach in search of wood in all kinds of weather, flapping about the rocks like some great bird with a damaged wing. She carried the messages down to the sea herself, growing more and more crazy and secretive every day. She paced the shore, her eyes watery and red-rimmed from scanning the empty horizon for the boat that never came. She shook her fist at Angus MacQueen, saying that the islanders were gathering up the letters and destroying them. "But you won't keep me shut up in yon stinking house forever!" she screamed. The only person she halfway trusted was Baine, who was slowly learning more words of her strange tongue and could now speak to her. Yet there were still times when she had no idea who the white-haired lad was.

The summers came and went, with the dark months in between. Catie turned thirteen and was growing tall, though not so tall as she wished to be. And as the time slipped by she almost felt in sympathy with Lady Grange, as if she, too, belonged to some other place. When she and Baine were up on the Neck of Cambir listening to the seals singing or surrounded by the wheeling birds on Conochair, she'd feel the other place quite close. But then Baine would ask her what she was seeing, and she could only find words for what was right there in front of her.

Baine was restless too. Climbing was in the islanders' blood. Lads of his age spent their days scaling the cliffs and bragging about their daring, and Baine raged at being left behind when they went off to snare guillemots and fulmars. He hated the tasks he was given instead—carding wool and plucking birds. "Women's work," he said angrily.

His mam didn't know what to do with him these days. Catie had heard her say as much to old Nan Finlay. Nan had been remarking on the way Baine went all over the island, even though he couldn't see.

"Next he'll be scrambling up the cliffs," she said.

"Nay, he'll never do that," Baine's mam answered, a shadow passing over her face. "And what joy is there in Hirta for a man who cannot climb?"

"At least *you'll* be spared some pain," Nan said. " 'Tis a terrible grief to hear the news that your own lad has fallen from the cliff. I'll never forget that day. I was standing in the doorway, there, and I looked up and saw these birds over Mullach Sgar . . ."

"He died a hero's death, Nan," Baine's mother interrupted gently. "You should be proud of his courage."

Catie wanted to tell Baine's mam that she should be proud of her own lad's courage, but she didn't dare. Wondering what it was like to be Baine, she had tried shutting her eyes while she stood on top of the dyke or walked along the shore, but they always sprung open the moment she felt herself falling or heard a wave roaring over the pebbles.

When she told Baine he was brave, it only made him angry. And no one—not even Catie herself—thought to tell the lad that his music was a gift to everyone. It nourished them as much as the bird flesh that the men brought home with such pride. They all loved to hear him sing, especially during the dark days. When the storage cleits were almost empty, his songs reminded them that the sun would shine again. He could sing a fractious bairn to sleep or turn an old man's thoughts to love. Yet Baine would have sat dumb around the fire if he could only have done men's work, weaving the wool into cloth and making the women new dresses. He'd tried hard to learn to weave, but the yarn tangled. Carding and spinning came more easily to his fingers.

And so Baine spent more and more time with Lady Grange, listening to her read from her black book and talk about the old days. He could never hear enough about the place called Edinburgh, with its castle as big as the island of Dun and a church steeple as high as Stac Lee. Lady Grange told him again and again about the cleverness of the good folk there, who could read and write and do all kinds of magic.

"Could they make me see?" he asked, turning the white-lashed eyes beseechingly toward her.

"They can do anything and everything," she answered.

Now it wasn't only Lady Grange who schemed and planned and dreamed of ways to reach Edinburgh.

"Why don't your friends in Edinburgh answer your letters?" Baine asked.

Lady Grange peered sideways through her long tangled hair. "They never get them," she whispered. "The people here don't want us to leave. I've seen them out in their boat picking up my messages."

"You could hide a letter in one of the bundles that goes to the mainland with the steward when he comes for the rent," Baine suggested.

"Aye, it might be that we can outdo them that way," Lady Grange agreed.

She tore the front page from her black book and lettered a message with more than usual care. Baine took the paper home and stuffed it deep inside a bundle of yarn his mam had set aside for the steward.

After the steward had come and gone, Baine told Catie about the letter in the yarn, and how Lady Grange had promised to take him to Edinburgh.

"You mustn't go with her, Baine," Catie said.

"There's people there who can make me see," he answered. "Then I'll come back to the island, and I'll climb up to the arch on Ruaival, and I'll stand on one foot, and . . ."

"And who will be your bride?" Catie asked.

"How can I tell you that until I can see!" Baine laughed.

Catie laughed too, though she didn't like this talk of Baine going away. Especially when he made her promise she'd help him when the boat came. But another year passed with the message still unanswered, so Catie stopped worrying.

Fog had shrouded Hirta for days, a thick, wet mist that dragged down everyone's spirits. Catie was wandering along the high tide mark looking for shells when she heard voices over by the jetty and the muffled splash of oars. None of the men would venture out in such weather. Besides, the Hirtans' boat was high and dry on the beach. Curious about what was happening, Catie hurried across the sand and scrambled over the rocks to the jetty. A small crowd had already gathered there.

"What's happening?" Catie asked breathlessly.

"They've finally come for Lady Grange," Niall Fergusson told her. "And now the poor daft woman doesn't want to go."

Anxiously Catie checked the crowd for Baine's white head and was glad to see he wasn't there. She watched the sailors drag Lady Grange onto the boat with about the same amount of respect as the other sailors had shown so many years before. Catie decided to wait until the boat was safely away from the island before she told Baine about this.

"They shouldn't go until the fog lifts," Niall said, shaking his head. "They'll never find their way in weather like this."

"Mainlanders are strange people," Angus Mac-Queen agreed as the boat cast off from the shore.

Instead of looking for Baine right away and breaking the news herself, Catie stopped to tell Anna and Dubh all about the boat in the fog and Lady Grange. Then she went home and told her mam. By the time she went to Baine's house, he'd already heard from someone else that Lady Grange had left the island.

"He took it badly," his mother said. "Though I think it's no loss that the poor crazy woman has finally been taken away. I never liked Baine spending so much time there. But now the lad's so upset that when he left the house he tripped and fell flat, though he knows the village like most of us know our own crub."

"Which way did he go?" Catie asked.

"He went up over the head dyke, but with the mist so thick I didn't see where he went from there. Go after him, Catie, lass, and bring him home."

Catie headed up the Big Stream and then over the pass to Gleann Mor. Several times she thought she heard him singing in the fog, but it was hard to place the direction of the sound. She picked her way across the marshy ground by the Well of Virtues and thought sadly how the water was claimed to cure any illness, but it hadn't given Baine his sight.

"Baine! Baine!" she shouted. "It's me! Catie! Come back, Baine!"

She ran on, and the fog was now so dense that she had to fight her way through it.

"Baine!" she screamed.

This time he answered. She heard his voice quite clearly.

"Caitlin! Caitlin! Where are you?"

The mist was growing thinner. From the springy feel of the turf under her bare feet, she could tell she was on the Cambir. On the Neck, close to the edge of the cliff.

"Baine!" she called again.

And again an answering call, quite close. "Caitlin!"

The mist parted and Dougal caught her in his arms.

17
ESCAPE

"LISTEN! DO YOU hear someone singing?" Caitlin asked, pulling away from Dougal's arms. Her face, so bleak only a moment before, was shining with hope. "I can hear him . . . over that way."

"It's just the seals, Caitlin. You often hear them up here on the Cambir."

"Of course . . . the seals," Caitlin repeated.

"Why did you run off last night?" Dougal's eyes, on a level with her own, were troubled. He wasn't good with words, and didn't seem sure how to go on. "The Old One woke up. She was afraid when you weren't there. She worries about you, Caitlin. She says you aren't like the rest of us."

You aren't like the rest of us.

The words brought Feadair's claim rushing back. Because she was so tall and her hair so long and straight . . . and red . . . she wasn't like the rest of them. In spite of anything Feadair said, she knew that

Tormod Rudh was her father. Had he not taught her how to climb and cared for her when she was a babe and no one else would do it? And now there was Dougal, who owed his very life to Tormod Rudh, repeating the Old One's gossiping hints.

"Where have you been, Caitlin?" Dougal asked. "Where did you go last night?"

"I'll tell you where I was!" Caitlin stormed. "I was walking around the circle with the druids. And my shadow fell across the stone. Across the sacrifice stone! Do you know what that means?"

For a moment Caitlin enjoyed the effect of her anger. It made her forget Feadair's lies, and poor blind Baine, lost forever in the mist.

But Dougal's face was so full of horror that Caitlin realized that there might be even more to fear than her worst imaginings.

"You—you don't know what you're saying," he stammered. "It can't be true!"

Caitlin closed her eyes to shut out his stricken look. Tears seeped through her lashes and ran down her cheeks.

"Caitlin, Caitlin," Dougal said, taking her in his arms again. "When the dark days come and the druids are enraged because there's not enough food on the island, you will be like a bird at the end of a fowler's snare, never knowing when the noose will be tightened. What are we going to do?"

"I'll find somewhere to hide," Caitlin said defiantly.

"Hide? On Hirta?" Dougal asked, letting her go.

Caitlin felt as if the noose were tightening already. Surely she could be safe up here on the Cambir . . . for a day or two . . . or she could live in a seal cave over on Dun. But what about food? If only the land still stretched all the way to the distant horizon . . .

Dougal was watching her, frowning the way he did when he was working out how to scale a cliff.

"How brave are you, lass?" he asked. "Or maybe it is a matter of how much you fear the druid's knife. Would you dare to spend the dark months all alone on Boreray? The Stallir would never find you there, and when you returned in the spring, he wouldn't dare touch you because you would have the spirits of Boreray on your side."

"The spirits of Boreray . . ." Caitlin whispered.

"They befriend anyone who lives there through the dark months alone. People often went there in the old days."

"It would be better than staying here . . . waiting . . ." Caitlin said. It would also put the sea between her and Feadair. "But how could I get there?"

"We can think about it."

Caitlin was the first to come up with an idea. "Maybe I could go along on the next gannet hunt," she suggested.

"If people are going to believe that the spirits on Boreray have a hand in your disappearance, we have to get you there without them knowing," Dougal answered. "Though you might be able to pass yourself off as Callum. He has no love for boats and wouldn't mind missing the trip. Can you handle an oar? They'd notice you if you didn't row."

"I could manage," Caitlin said.

"Aye, but how will you manage once you're there?"

"There are sheep on Boreray. I'll be able to get milk until the lambs are weaned," Caitlin said eagerly. "And I can snare puffins and dry them for winter."

"If you were in trouble, you could turn over a piece of turf on the southwest pasture and send news the way we do when we're hunting gannets there in the summer," Dougal said, warming to the plan.

"What use would a signal be if the wind was blowing and you couldn't launch the boat?" Caitlin asked.

"I'd think of something," Dougal promised. "The most important thing in a storm is shelter—and there's the Stallir house for that. We'll take some sheepskins for you to wrap yourself in."

Caitlin shivered at the mention of the druids' house, but she wasn't going to let Dougal see that she was afraid.

The islanders usually went after gannets under the cover of darkness on a moonless night. The birds slept on high ledges above the sea, with a sentinel bird keeping watch, soothing the sleeping birds with soft sounds. *Grog, grog, grog.* All is well. All is well. If the sentinel bird sensed danger, the cry changed to a high *birr birr*, and the whole flock would take to the air. The first man down to the ledges silently killed the sentinel bird, allowing the rest of the hunters to take as many of the sleeping birds as they needed, all the while keeping up the sentinel's soothing call, *Grog, grog, grog*.

Caitlin counted off the days of summer with a mixture of fear and longing. When the nights began to grow longer, she watched the passing phases of the moon. One calm afternoon, all the men were down on the beach testing ropes and getting the boat ready, and she knew that her wait was over.

"Tonight?" she whispered to Dougal, catching up with him on his way down to the beach.

"Aye, if the weather stays fine," Dougal said. "That light fog will muffle the sound of the oars and make the night darker, but if it gets thicker, we could lose our bearings and wreck the boat on one of the stacs or row wide of the island."

Caitlin kept an anxious eye on the weather all day. Late in the afternoon, when the Old One had gone up to the well, she hurriedly gathered what she would need. She didn't like leaving the old woman without any parting words, but Dougal said that was how it must be. On hearing footsteps outside the house, she stuffed her bundle under the sheepskin on the crub, but it turned out to be Dougal.

"Ready, lass?" he asked.

"Aye," Caitlin answered, retrieving the bundle and

tying it to her belt. "I have a firestone and a good piece of hide rope."

"I'll let you have this," Dougal said, taking off his own thick cloak. "It'll keep out the storm winds better than that old one you have. And for goodness' sake, pull the hood up over your head! No one else has hair like yours."

On the way down to the shore through the gathering darkness, Dougal had more to say than usual. "Remember not to speak," he warned Caitlin. "Even though Callum's voice is still high, you don't curse like he does when things go amiss! And if someone does notice you, we'll say nothing about you staying on Boreray—just that you wanted to see the gannet hunt. But there'll be a terrible fuss. A woman on the boat brings bad luck and we'll have to turn back."

"When we go over to Boreray for the lambing, there are always women on the boat," Caitlin said.

"And almost always a storm blows up."

Caitlin could have pointed out that the storms blew up because the lambing came in the spring, when the weather was unpredictable, but it wasn't worth arguing over. Besides, it was time to think about jumping into the boat.

"Hurry up!" Gareth shouted.

Dougal went first and Caitlin grabbed an oar as he pulled her down onto the seat in front of him. The oar felt heavy and awkward in her hand, but by the time they were a couple of boat lengths from the shore, she'd caught the rhythm. She began to feel exhilarated as the distance between the boat and Hirta widened, though her exhilaration was already tinged with loneliness.

Gareth warned them to be quiet as they approached the cliffs of Boreray. There was no good landing place below the gannets' nests, so he was going to stay with the boat while the others leaped across the black water to a narrow ledge on the face of the cliff. All of them—except Caitlin—held a picture of the rock in their minds from other times. Nimble as she was, Caitlin was caught off balance by the bundle tied at her waist. She would have slipped if Dougal hadn't grabbed her and held her against the rock.

"Veer to the right and keep climbing," he whispered. "You'll find a small cleft in the cliff face, where I'll leave you an extra sheepskin. Hide in there until we're at the top and then you can find your own way up."

18

BORERAY

THE NEXT MORNING, when the sun was high, Caitlin watched with a feeling of triumph as the boat left Boreray. She had escaped from Hirta, leaving all her worries behind. She only needed to catch enough birds to feed herself. The Stallir couldn't reach her here with his demands at the Feast of Samain. Nor could Feadair. He couldn't take Tormod Rudh away from her here. She would climb the rocks and snare birds the way her father had taught her. On Boreray she would be at peace with the world. The heather bloomed for no other eyes than hers; a friendly wren serenaded her from an outcrop. Her lips and teeth were soon stained with the juice of the tiny blueberries she gathered as she went exploring. After setting her puffin snares near the crowded burrows, she chose a cleit on the sloping sheep pasture facing Hirta to store her sheepskin, her cloak, and her bag of tools and rope. While she gathered stones to build a pen to hold one or two sheep at milking time, she wondered if Dougal was up at the Gap gazing over at Boreray.

For as long as the sun shone Caitlin gloried in being alone. But late in the afternoon of the fifth day, the wind picked up and purple clouds loomed over Hirta. Feeling the wind's sharp edge, Caitlin took refuge in the cleit, but even huddled inside her sheepskin cloak she still shivered. This was only a late-summer storm. What would life be like when the dark days came, she wondered uneasily. The puffins would be leaving soon, and she hadn't nearly enough meat to last the winter. Unless there were several more days of hot sunshine, the birds that were already drying would rot. Caitlin stared out across the water at the dark, ragged shape of Hirta. Summer was slipping away like fine sand between her fingers, but she knew that when the cold months came, time would stand still.

Higher up in the pasture, the Stallir house was a smooth green nob on the hill. It was silly to shiver in a drafty cleit when she could take shelter in the underground house and be out of the wind, yet another hour passed before she had the courage to leave the cleit. At last, crouching against the slanting rain, she scuttled up the hillside. When she reached the low doorway—like a dark mouth opening into the hill—she stopped. Would the Stallir know she was there, even from far away on Hirta? Lightning forked across the sky, followed by a roll of thunder. Caitlin crawled through the entry tunnel.

When her eyes finally adjusted to the dim light filtering down through the wide smoke hole in the roof, she was amazed at the size of the room. It was bigger than anything on Hirta and deeper underground. The sleeping crubs in the walls were like yawning caves above the stone benches that encircled the room. Now that she was actually inside, her fear was manageable, but the idea of spending the night in this place was too awful to think about. The spirit of the druids permeated the earthen walls and the corbelled ceiling. She could almost hear the music of Feadair's harp and the low voice of the seer telling stories from the time beyond. Perhaps if she built a fire, the voices would go away. And she needed fulmar oil for a lamp—but she wasn't sure she could catch a fulmar by herself. Caitlin's eyes brimmed with tears. Dougal had overestimated her skill when he thought that she could live alone on Boreray, but even worse, he had overestimated her courage.

"A fire! The first thing to do is light a fire," she said aloud.

Her voice echoed strangely, but she felt better when she found a store of dried grass and heather twigs and a stack of peat inside the door. She brought a handful of kindling over to the fire pit and built it into a loose mound like a cleit. Then she reached into her pouch for the firestone. Once the fire was going, she shoved in more twigs of heather and dry bracken to feed the flame. Fire lived longer in glowing peat, but the dancing flames assured her that it was really alive. She rubbed her fingers to chafe the coldness out of them, then cupped her hands around the flame. For almost the first time since Feadair had claimed he was her father, she let herself think about what this meant. She was part druid—she belonged here—and from her druid self came the power to reach the time beyond.

She stared into the flame. Could she make it happen again? And if she could, would she go back to Erik . . . or to Baine? No, she would go instead to Brendan's time. Before the Vikings came, Brendan had somehow defeated the spirits of the afterworld. He had come with a message of peace that had changed Hirta, holding the islanders together even when his words were imperfectly remembered. But if she could just hear the story from his own lips. . . .

Caitlin shook herself. She was falling under the druids' spell—imagining she could escape because she was part druid. Tormod Rudh was her father! Had he not taught her to climb the cliffs and snare birds? It was Tormod's skills that would save her—not druid magic.

All the same, when the storm finally blew itself out, she trapped only a few more birds, and the number of carcasses drying in the sun and strung up around the fire remained pitifully small. She ate blueberries and sorrel and drank ewe's milk. One evening she found an abandoned nest of eggs, and fell asleep for the first time in many days with her stomach comfortably full.

Soon the puffins were gone and Caitlin missed their comical antics. She watched the fulmars testing the wind, impatient to be on their way, too. Even the gleaming gannets that flew home so purposefully each evening would soon forsake Boreray.

The days grew shorter than the nights.

One afternoon Caitlin climbed to the sheep pasture, the wind making streamers of her hair and tugging at her woolen shift. She gazed out toward Hirta. How long had they searched when they first missed her? Did the Old One think she had gone over the cliff, or did she know Caitlin was here on Boreray? The Old One had a way of knowing.

And what about Dougal? Had he really thought she could spend the dark months on Boreray alone? Would he come for her if she dug up a patch of turf on the pasture? Maybe he was on the Gap now, thinking of her. Or maybe this was his way of punishing her for deserting him on the night of the Beltane fire. She pushed that thought away and tried instead to hold on to the feeling of his arms around her for that brief moment on the Cambir. Remembering his strength and his quietness, she missed him so much that when she spoke of her longing aloud her words matched the music of one of Cathan's love songs.

"Let the winds carry my song
   Like the fulmar riding the air;
Let the waves carry my words

Like the drifting foam.
My song is the wind, my tears the ocean,
Come, Beloved, come!"

She was singing! She had made poetry—with none but the sheep to hear! Now she could while away the dark months with songs of Tormod Rudh, but even as she planned this a small doubt crept into her mind. Perhaps she was part druid after all. She pushed the thought away. There had been no poetry in her last winter. The gift of singing had been learned from Cathan in the time beyond. She sang her song again, louder, because the wind was throwing the words back at her.

The gannets were streaming home to their roosting ledges and dark clouds were building over Hirta—both sure signs that a change in the weather was near. Below, the ocean was slate gray and flecked with the white crests of waves. Caitlin narrowed her eyes. Something was bobbing around on the water, closer to Boreray than to Hirta but still a long way out. Perhaps there was magic in her song! Dougal must have heard her singing and was coming to rescue her. But the thing in the water wasn't big enough to be the boat and it moved too randomly. Yet as it drew closer she saw that it was indeed some kind of vessel, round and so light that the waves were playing with it, each wave picking it up and tossing it to the wave behind.

Caitlin slithered down the steep hillside, making for

the cleit where she'd left her rope. Judging from the direction of the wind and the waves, the boat would end up near the place they'd landed on the night of no moon. With the rope coiled over her shoulder, she scrambled down the rocks and braced herself in the narrow cleft where she'd spent her first hours on Boreray. From there she watched the boat. Even from a distance she sensed that the solitary oarsman didn't have the skill to bring the boat in safely against the sheer cliff—though it might not be so much the man's fault as the design of the boat.

The next wave lifted the little round coracle, spinning it about while the man made ineffectual stabs with his oar. Caitlin watched, all the while wondering if this was more druid magic. A stranger had not come to these shores in all her days. But when she looked into her mind, it was her own life that she found there. Nothing had changed. She was still Caitlin, alone on Boreray. Caitlin, whose shadow had darkened the sacrifice stone on midsummer's morn on Conochair. Caitlin, the daughter of Tormod Rudh, she reminded herself firmly.

She turned her attention back to the man and the boat. His only chance was to jump, and she was hoping that when the boat hit the rocks, it wouldn't be smashed so completely that everything was lost. Caitlin cautiously lowered herself farther down the cliff, knowing that whatever was washed up by one wave was invariably taken by the next. The man seemed to have given up. He had thrown down his oar and was now kneeling in the bottom of the tossing boat, his hands clasped close to his chest. The wind had torn back his brown hood, revealing a smooth, bald head with a fringe of gray hair. For a moment the clouds parted and a shaft of sunlight lit up his face—a thin face, almost hairless, which was strange in a man so old. But the most remarkable thing of all was that it was the face of a man who was not afraid.

19

THE STRANGER

BECAUSE THE MAN was without fear, Caitlin couldn't bear to see him smash against the rocks. She deftly looped her rope around a nob in the crevice above her head and hurled the loose coil down to the tossing boat. The stranger managed to grab the rope on the second try, but he wouldn't let Caitlin pull him up the cliff. Though she couldn't hear a word he said over the crashing surf, she knew he didn't want to abandon the boat. He was waving her away. He no doubt wanted her to fetch someone to help her. But there's no one else, she thought grimly as he let the rope slither through his hands and the boat was sucked back out to sea.

The next wave brought him close to the wall of rock again, and she yelled to him to jump at the height of the wave. He was a fool for coming in so close if he didn't intend to jump. His skin boat didn't stand a chance on these rocks. As if able to read Caitlin's mind, the man picked up his feeble oar to push the boat away. Frantic at the thought of losing the only person she'd seen in all the changes of the moon, Caitlin swung farther down the cliff, and jerking her rope free, she jumped for the boat at the very instant the man should have jumped for the shore.

It was nearly the end of both of them. The frail coracle tipped so that empty air was under them and the wall of water that was the next wave became the sky. Miraculously the boat righted itself, riding up the wave. Caitlin lay in the bottom of the boat clinging to the heap of rope, shaking. Although the rope was attached to nothing, it was still something to hold on to. The man was trying to row now, and though it was hard to be sure, he did appear to be maneuvering the tiny vessel away from the cliff. His strength seemed to come from his words, words that he sang out in a voice that rivaled the winds.

> "The Lord is a great God and a great
>   King above all gods.
> In his hand are the deep places of the
>   earth: the strength of the hills is his also.
> The sea is his, and he made it: and his
>   hands formed the dry land."

The boat spun around again. Caitlin's stomach heaved and she was sick. For a time her courage left her altogether. She would almost have welcomed the splintering sound of the boat's frame against the rocks and the roar of water in her ears as the boat sank. Anything to stop the mad rush up the waves followed by the drop into nothingness, with her stomach rising each time the boat fell. After a stretch of time that seemed to last forever, Caitlin was able to raise her head. A dark expanse of water now separated them from Boreray. The boat still rocked crazily, but the waves weren't quite so unpredictable away from the land. The man was talking to her, and although his voice was strange, she finally made sense of what he was saying. He was asking her the name of the island.

"Boreray," she answered.

"How many people live there?"

"I was alone."

"How many others?"

"None."

When she began to explain why, to her surprise he nodded. He knew about the druids and even understood about her shadow on the stone.

"We have druids on the Green Island too, but they have learned that there is no more need for sacrifice," he said, his thin face glowing. "God sent his Son to live among us and he was sacrificed for all our sins."

"But winter isn't here yet . . . the time of darkness and storms and hunger . . ."

Caitlin tried to find the right words to explain, but finally she gave up. The storm was all she could deal with for now. As the stretch of water between them and Boreray gradually grew wider, and their distance from Hirta less, the looming cliffs of Conochair brought all of Caitlin's fears rushing back. The man handed her a pan to bail out the water that was threatening to swamp the boat, but that did nothing for the thoughts that were swamping her mind. What had been happening on Hirta while she'd been gone? Would the Stallir be waiting for her? And Feadair? Her own people would be angry that she'd stolen a ride to Boreray. They'd be quick to put the blame on her for anything that had gone wrong.

The stranger had stopped rowing and was gazing at the awesome cliffs rising straight from the sea. The restless waves and swiftly moving clouds made the cliffs appear as if they too were caught in the mad dance. And Caitlin knew that somewhere close to the edge of the cliff the druid circle of stones stood silently waiting—twelve standing stones and one lying flat. Soon it would be time for the Samain feast, and she and the Old One would have almost nothing to give.

The wind was gusting strongly again. With more luck than skill the man maneuvered the boat along the bottom of the cliffs and safely around the headland of Oiseval, only to go scudding straight across Village Bay toward the merciless rocks of Dun, with no hope of landing on the beach. Above the screaming wind Caitlin could hear him shouting, "They cry unto the Lord in their trouble, and he bringeth them out of their distresses." But his words weren't any help. The waves were breaking over the side of the boat while he struggled hopelessly to steer toward the beach, his oar no more effective than a feather. Caitlin began to bail again, but the wind dashed the water back into her face. For an endless time, they made no progress at all. Then Caitlin saw the stac that guarded the Dun Gap rearing up directly ahead.

The stranger's voice rolled on. "He maketh the storm a calm, so that the waves thereof are still."

The boat hung on the top of a wave while the jagged tooth lunged at them. Caitlin could see the runnels of water from the last wave pouring down the barnacle-studded rock. The next wave carried them into the Gap on the Hirta side, where someone was moving, crablike down the face of the cliff. There seemed to be no way the person could reach them in time.

"Help! Help us!" Caitlin screamed.

People were running frantically along the edge of the cliff top. And behind them stood a solitary druid, like a tall white stone against the dark backdrop of Ruaival. The tossing boat and salt spray and the distance from the shore made it impossible for Caitlin to tell if it was Feadair or the Stallir or some other druid who had chanced to be passing that way, yet for a moment she seemed to look directly into his eyes. Dark, cold eyes. Then everything was noise and confusion, as the next wave broke right over the boat, submerging Caitlin in the dark coldness of the water.

The silence that followed the roaring inside her head was interrupted by an insistent voice saying, "He's alive, I tell you! He's alive! I saw his eyelids flutter."

It was her own voice.

She was standing on the rocks, peering into the waxen face of a half-drowned stranger. Some man she'd never set eyes on before. He was bearded, with thick brown hair plastered against his head. Blood oozed from a cut on his temple, and his near-naked body was scraped and bruised.

Beside her another man, dressed completely in black except for a gleaming white band around his neck, was chanting in a monotonous voice, "He maketh the storm a calm, so that the waves thereof are still."

The words had a familiar ring, but the half-drowned stranger was all she could think about just now.

20

CATRIONA

"GO ON UP to the house, lass, and tell them that we're bringing home a half-drowned sailor. Have Ma build up the fire and put on a pot of broth."

She hesitated, not wanting to leave the sailor's side until she was sure that he was going to live, but her father repeated impatiently, "Get along with you, Catriona! Run!"

With the wind at her back, she was practically blown from the shore to the village, but when she reached the street, a flagstone causeway with houses along one side, their windows facing out to the bay, she stopped in confusion. It was as if she were seeing it for the first time: the hewn stone cottages, with chimneys atop each gable, and the tarred felt roofs tied down with stout ropes against the wind. But when she stepped inside the door of Number Three, everything seemed familiar again. The box bed, the barrel of salted sea birds by the door, and the table under the window where the visitor spent all his time writing. Now he would have something to write about!

Her mother looked up from her knitting when the girl burst into the room. "What's wrong, Catriona?" she asked, her voice tight with anxiety.

"A big steamer was driven against the rocks of Dun," Catriona answered breathlessly. "They've saved nine men, and Father's bringing one of them here. He's badly hurt—"

"Your father's hurt, lass?" her mother interrupted.

"Not Father! It's the sailor who is hurt. He was washed up on the rocks, and his clothes were ripped right off him! At first they thought he had no life in him, but they thumped the water out of him anyway, and then I saw him flutter his eyelids and I knew he wasn't dead. Mr. Mackay, the minister, was there, too, telling the storm to quiet down."

"And what about the state of the others?" Catriona's mother asked, crossing the room to peer out the small window, although she could see nothing through the driving rain. She was a bonny woman with a clear complexion and black hair parted neatly in the middle and worn in braids looped together at the back of her head.

"The others are all better off than our one," Catriona said.

"Our one, indeed." Her mother sniffed. "Have we not got enough to do with the visitor staying here?"

"He'll hear you!" Catriona said.

Then she realized that their visitor, John Sands from the mainland, was not at his usual place. Unlike all the other visitors that came on the steamer in the summertime, he had stayed on through the dark months. Day after day he sat at the table by the window, writing a book about life on the St. Kilda Islands, which was what he called Hirta, Soay, Boreray, and Dun. He wrote by the light of the fulmar-oil lamp until late in the evening, though no one could fathom how he found so much to say.

"Mr. Sands went over to Grannie MacCrimmon's to listen to her blether about the old days and to ask about things best forgotten," Catriona's mother said.

Although it would have meant missing out on the biggest event on Hirta all winter, Catriona was almost sorry she hadn't gone with the visitor. She liked to hear Grannie sing the old songs. "I wonder if she sang him the one about the seals luring the people off the cliff," she said. "How they floated on the wind until the waves reached up and got them."

"Hush, Catriona!" her mother said in a shocked voice. "Have you not heard Mr. Mackay say often enough that the old singing and dancing are tainted by the devil? The minister is a learned man from the mainland, and knows about such things. But we shouldn't be standing here blethering ourselves. Take Fiona with you and fetch more peat for the fire."

Little Fiona climbed off the box bed, where she'd been amusing herself with her sea shells, and came running across the room. She was a solemn child with a great mop of dark curls. The two girls skipped off, unmindful of the wind and rain. Each girl fetched a hod of peat from the stack behind the house, hoisting the heavy load onto her back. The women on Hirta had always done the carrying—hay for the cattle, dung for the fields, peat for the fire. This was one of the old ways that the learned minister saw no reason to change.

By the time the kettle was boiling, the men had come up from the beach with the sailor. They laid him, moaning and grumbling, on the box bed, but Catriona could hardly get a glimpse of him with so many others crowded around. Some of the neighbors, who had no sailors of their own to look after, had dropped by to join in the excitement. Catriona's grandfather, after one look at the poor man, went rummaging in the trunk at the back of the room. He lifted out the suit of dark blue cloth he'd made last winter.

"Put this on him to cover his nakedness," he said, shaking the suit from its folds and handing it to Catriona's father.

"But that's your new suit, Father!" Catriona's mother protested. "The one you said you'd be buried in."

"Have you not heard the words of the Reverend Mackay, taken straight from the Book?" the old man asked. "He that hath two coats, let him impart to him that hath none; he that hath meat, let him do likewise."

"I just hope you won't need the suit yourself before spring," Ma said sourly.

The thought of the empty storage cleits behind the house made Catriona's mother sharp-tongued these days. Last summer the barley crop had been battered by storms, and the fulmar harvest had been poor. The sugar and tea and tobacco and bonnets and cravats that the steward had brought from the mainland in exchange for their feathers and tweed didn't fill hungry stomachs. Or maybe it was the memory of the new bairn that had been taken by "the sickness of eight days" last spring that had silenced her laughter. At any rate, it was easy to see that she wasn't happy at the thought of another mouth to feed, though she was ladling some thin gruel into her best bowl.

It was long past bedtime, but Catriona and Fiona were wide awake, sitting on the edge of the hearth at old Grannie MacCrimmon's feet. Grannie's shoes, peeking out from under her long skirt, were made from gannet skins turned inside out so that the down was against her feet. No one else on the island wore gannet shoes nowadays, but Grannie stuck to the old ways. Even so, she liked to know everything that was going on, and she had left her own fire to come over to see the sailor with her own eyes. A shipwreck, in the dark months when the St. Kildans never saw a stranger, provided so much to talk about that the men couldn't wait until the morning parliament to begin going over all that had happened, so Catriona and Fiona and old Grannie were able to keep abreast of the news.

". . . And the ship's captain is staying at the manse, along with two of the crew."

". . . One man was wearing one sock that was red, and the other blue . . ."

"Nan Gillies cooked up a pot of porridge, scraping the last oats from the bin and . . ."

Words swirled around the room, everyone eager to have their say, but when the visitor came in, shaking the rain off his oilskins like a wet dog, they all fell quiet.

"Have you spoken with the other sailors, Mr. Sands?" Catriona's father asked politely.

"As well as I was able," Mr. Sands answered. "They don't speak much English."

"You mean to say they have the Gaelic?"

"German, I think."

This news took a while to sink in.

"Their boat was named the *Peti Dubrovacki,* and they're from Austria," the visitor continued.

"Austria! Then you must ask them if they know Ewen Gillies."

Liam MacDonald was all for rousing the miserable sailor in the box bed to find out right away. Despite the commotion in the room, he was dozing fitfully.

"Ewen Gillies?" Mr. Sands repeated.

"Aye, our Ewen went there more than twenty years ago."

"Twenty years is a long time," the visitor said. "And there's a lot of people in Austria. No one could know them all."

"They'd know our Ewen," Finlay Gillies said confidently. "He found gold and came back to tell us. Ewen went all around the world . . . fought in a big war in America and then found more gold in California. California Gillies, we named him when he came home."

"Maybe it was Australia where Ewen went . . ."

"That's what we were telling you," Finlay broke in impatiently.

"The sailors are from Austria," Mr. Sands explained. "It's not the same place."

Once again the conversation ebbed and flowed. People argued over the foolishness of giving two places almost the same name, and others marveled that Ewen could go off and find gold and fight in a war and be forgotten so soon. They told each other that it must be strange to live in a place where you could meet a person on the street and not stop to shake his hand. Imagine meeting a man and not knowing what name to call him!

And then the conversation took another turn.

"With their boat smashed on the rocks, they'll be with us till the first steamer comes in the summer," Catriona's mother said.

"How are we going to feed them?" Rachel Gillies asked. "We're already scraping the bottom of our oat barrel."

"Have you not heard God's word in the Book, woman?" Grandfather thundered. "Behold the fowls of the air: for they sow not, neither do they reap, nor gather into barns; yet your heavenly Father feedeth them. Are ye not much better than they?"

"The good Lord is going to have to work a miracle," Catriona's mother snapped.

"Maybe He'll send us calm weather, and we can go out after fish," Liam suggested.

No one spoke for a moment, and the sound of a dog barking and the wind rattling the door and whining in the chimney filled the silence.

On Saturday night the wind dropped, and Sunday dawned fine. Catriona wiped the soot and condensation from the small windowpane with the hem of her skirt and looked out at the clear sky, pinkish in the dawn. Fine days were few and far between at this time of the year. It was too bad that God had sent one on the Sabbath, when they had to spend the day in church listening to the minister, with no chance of taking the boat out in the bay or combing the beach for anything washed up by the storm. These last few days, the waves had been so wild that they hadn't been able to do a good job of scavenging the debris from the wreck. And tomorrow the weather would likely change again.

Catriona knew better than to voice any of these ungodly thoughts to her mother and father. The Sabbath was a day of silence, the only words spoken aloud being words from the Book. The cows had been milked the night before and would stay in the byre till Monday morning. Cooking and mending nets and weaving cloth—anything that would take their minds from thoughts of God—were all forbidden. But Catriona's mind had a way of wandering to forbidden subjects even more when she was idle.

Their sailor was already up and about, and Catriona was glad to discover that it wasn't a sin for him and the other sailors to go down on the beach on the Sabbath, though later in the day the minister set them right on that. He said the time would come when the sailors wished that they were again being battered by the cold Atlantic instead of spending all eternity roasting in the fires of hell.

Catriona and Fiona and their mother and father and grandfather were seated in their pew near the front of the church long before the bell rang to mark the beginning of the morning service. Wee Fiona could sit as still as a nesting bird for two hours or more, but Catriona, though older, earned more than one scowl from her father for swinging her legs or shifting in her seat or rustling the pages of her Bible. Once—close to a year ago—the minister had stopped his sermon and pointed his finger at Catriona. The elder had come to their house that afternoon and tested her in the catechism. Fortunately her memory was good and he pronounced that she wouldn't end up in hell if from that day on she remembered to sit still in church and pay heed to the minister speaking the Word of God.

While they were singing the hundred and nineteenth psalm, Catriona noticed that Grannie MacCrimmon's pew was empty. She must be sick. Catriona pictured her sitting in the smoky darkness of her little black house, or maybe lying in a tangle of blankets in the crub. Grannie had been old even back in the early 1860s when John MacLeod, the proprietor, had built all of them new houses with chimneys to let out the smoke and windows to let in the light. But Grannie MacCrimmon had refused to leave her old black house, and Catriona didn't altogether blame her. The rounded corners and the double stone walls with sod and rubble packed between kept her house snug against the wind. In the new houses there were nights when the wild wind shrieked like a wailing banshee and no one could sleep. The smoke was blown back down the new-fangled chimney pots so that the white walls were already dark with soot. The roofs of zinc sheeting had long since been blown away and replaced by tarred felt criss-crossed with ropes to anchor it. But the rooms were of a good size, and it was a great thing to be able to look out of the glass windows. Moreover,

MacLeod had given them chairs and tables made of wood, and chests and Bibles. And even before they had new houses a minister had been sent out from the mainland to care for their souls and to teach them to read so that they might know the Scriptures of the Lord.

The minister was talking about the sailors again. It seemed that God had sent them to Hirta to test the people. "Lord, when saw we thee hungry and fed thee?" the minister asked in his thundering voice. "Or thirsty, and gave thee drink? When saw we thee a stranger and took thee in? Or naked, and clothed thee? Or when we saw thee sick, or in prison, and came unto thee? And the King shall answer and say unto them, Verily I say unto you, inasmuch as ye have done it unto one of the least of these my brethren, ye have done it unto me."

But it wasn't going to be easy to feed the hungry when they themselves were hungry. Catriona could remember how it had been last spring before the birds came back. It was going to be worse this year with nine extra men and the visitor, all with big appetites. The sailor and the visitor had had porridge and salted fulmars for breakfast that morning, while all she'd had was a drink of milk.

Now Mr. Mackay was talking about visiting the sick, and Catriona began to fret about Grannie again. Maybe she could slip away and see her this afternoon while Grandfather was reading from the Book. Sometimes he got so carried away with the sound of his own voice that he forgot there was anyone listening. And the minister himself was saying that visiting the sick was like laying up good fortune in heaven.

Yes, she'd slip over and see Grannie MacCrimmon that very afternoon!

21
GRANNIE MACCRIMMON

WHEN CATRIONA DISCOVERED that Grannie MacCrimmon's house was dark and empty, she was worried. She ran outside and looked up and down the length of the street, Sabbath-solemn and without a soul about. What could have happened to Grannie? Maybe she had gone up to St. Brendan's Church on Ruaival. All that was left of the old building were the stone walls and a scattering of bones—whale ribs that had long ago supported the sod roof—but Grannie liked to go up there by herself. Catriona waded across the Big Stream, clambered over the village dyke, then headed up the hill.

She found the old woman sitting on a fallen stone by the low wall, her plaid covering her head and shoulders, and her brown, veined hands gripping the peeled staff that went with her everywhere. The shadowed face under the plaid was grooved and wrinkled, but the dark eyes watching Catriona were bright.

"I thought you were sick, Grannie," Catriona shouted when she was close enough to be heard.

"And so you're sorry to find me well?" Grannie asked.

Catriona grinned. "The minister said in church this morning for us to visit the sick . . . but if you're not sick, then I'd better be off home."

She knew how to tease, too.

"Sit down, lass, now that you're here," Grannie said, making room for Catriona beside her. "It won't hurt you to stay and listen to the voice of Brendan for a little. Long, long ago, our destiny lay in his hands."

"If he lived so long ago, how can we hear him now?" Catriona asked.

"The spirits of our forebears speak to us from the rocks and waterfalls, if you would just listen. The deeds of the past are thick around us."

"The minister says that the spirits are all in heaven— or in hell."

"I'm thinking that the minister doesn't know everything."

"Grannie!" Catriona said, scandalized.

"Just like the MacLeods didn't know everything when they put up those newfangled houses down there. They'd never spent the dark months on Hirta or they'd have known those zinc roofs would blow away in the first gale."

"That was before I was even born, Grannie," Catriona said impatiently. "I've never seen a roof blow off!"

"Aye, but you've sat under many a leak. And when the roof needs mending, we cannot do it ourselves, but have to ask Mr. MacLeod to send us stuff from the mainland to fix it. If a man cannot keep a roof over his own family's head, what does that do to his pride? Each year we trade our feathers and oil for more things that we do not need, and then think we cannot do without them."

"But I like when the steamers come in, Grannie," Catriona argued. "Last year one of the visitors gave Fiona and me each a penny with Queen Victoria's head on it. Father made them into brooches for us, and we've got them still."

"Long ago, in my mother's day, there was more pride among our people," Grannie MacCrimmon said, looking off into the distance. "The men were more daring, living out their lives close to death. In those days a man proved his courage on the Mistress Stone before taking a wife, and there was singing and dancing at the wedding."

The minister didn't hold with singing and dancing, but Catriona had already broken so many rules this Sabbath day that it didn't worry her at all when the old woman began to sing.

"Away, bent spade, away, straight spade,
Away, each goat and sheep and lamb;

Up my rope, up my snare—
I have heard the gannet upon the sea!
Thanks to the Being, the gannets are come,
Yes, and the big birds along with them;
Dark, dusky maid, a cow in the fold!
A brown cow, a brown cow, a brown cow
   beloved,
A brown cow, my dear one, that would
   milk the milk for thee.
Ho ro ru ra ree, playful maid,
Dark, dusky maid, cow in the fold!
The birds are a-coming, I hear their tune!"

The words were cheerful enough, but the melody was so strangely haunting that Catriona was left feeling happy and sad at the same time.

"That's pretty, Grannie," she whispered. "Where did you learn it?"

"It's one of blind Baine's songs. In the old days we sang his tunes all the time. I can remember the women singing as they walked over to Gleann Mor to do the ewe milking, and the sound of the men's voices drifting up from the bay when they brought in the boat from the fishing."

"Tell me about blind Baine."

"Back at the time my granny was young, a white-haired bairn was born," Grannie said softly. "Day and night were the same to the poor bairn because he could not tell the light from the dark. But the wee folk cared for him, and gave him the gift of song. They even showed him how to find his way about the island, judging his place by the cries of the birds and the voice of the wind. But one day, when he was up on the Cambir, the fog rolled in, smothering sound, and Baine lost his bearings—just as a sighted person does in a fog. He went over the cliff."

"Could the faeries not have saved him?"

Grannie shook her head. "Some say that it was the spite of the faerie folk that made it happen. You see, he'd fallen in love with a human lass. Have you never heard them singing?"

"But you said Baine lived 'way back when your granny was a bairn."

"Standing on the Neck of the Cambir, you can hear blind Baine and his lass Catie blending their voices in harmony with the music of the seals down in the sea. Catie was frightened that day when she saw the fog, and went looking for Baine. She too was lured over the cliff, on the east side of the Neck. But even the faerie folk cannot keep the two from meeting now. If you go up on the Cambir on a fine day you will hear their voices, and the music is not of this world."

"I've heard them, Grannie," Catriona whispered. "I thought it was just the seals down in the water."

"Nay, lass, it is the voices of Baine and Catie, and when you hear them, they are together and happy that you have united them again. They lived on Hirta at the same time as Lady Grange."

Although Catriona had heard the tale of the poor crazy woman and her letters tied to bits of wood before, she didn't mind hearing Grannie tell it once again.

"She must have been right happy when that boat came to take her home," Catriona said when the story was finished.

"Aye," Grannie answered. "But her happiness was short-lived. You see, her husband had heard about the letter she'd sent, and it was his boat that reached the island first. He took her over to Skye and hid her away again. It was there she died—twelve long years a prisoner, poor soul!"

The silence that followed Grannie's story was broken by the peal of the church bell calling the people to their evening worship.

"We should be down there!" Catriona said, jumping to her feet, her eyes wide with fright. "They'll have missed me by now—I'll be in awful trouble. Mr. Mackay will denounce me from the pulpit, Grannie, if I walk in late, but it will be worse if I don't go at all."

"I'll come down with you, lass," Grannie MacCrimmon said. "Trouble shared is trouble halved."

The old woman, leaning on her staff, made her way so slowly down the rough hillside that Catriona thought the trouble would more likely be doubled, but all the same she wanted to have Grannie at her side when she walked into the church. Besides, if she ran on ahead, Grannie might not come at all.

"Do you not worry about not going to heaven— missing the service this morning and now being late?" Catriona asked, looking anxiously at Grannie's wrinkled face. Grannie was old enough that she should be considering such things.

"I'm not sure that I'd be comfortable in heaven— I'd look right foolish floating about like a gannet on the wind. No, I'd rather my spirit stayed here in Hirta, living on in a rock or in the waterfall. That's what they thought before the learned men from the mainland told us differently, and that's what I would still believe. When you've lived as long as I have, lass, you become a part of Hirta, and even heaven in all its glory could not compare with what we have here."

"When I'm with you, hearing the old stories, I feel like I am part of the island too," Catriona said, reaching out and taking Grannie's hand, thin and hard like a bird's claw.

Still hand-in-hand, they walked down the aisle of the church. The minister stopped speaking when they came in and a terrible silence settled over the whole congregation. Catriona's face was red and her heart was hammering like a snared puffin's. She slid into her pew next to Fiona. Grannie stomped on down to her own pew, leaning heavily on her staff.

The minister took a deep breath and resumed the service, his voice rolling out the words, "Tonight I will take the text of my sermon from the story of the Prodigal Son."

22
THE ST. KILDA MAILBOAT

"MAYBE THE BIRDS will return early this spring!"

Ma's plaintive words echoed back through the years. Always, toward the end of the dark days, the lean times cramped their stomachs and had the men plaiting snares and testing ropes in readiness for the first birds, but this year, with the sailors and the visitor to feed, the lean time had come sooner. The sailors, who had not been conditioned by the hungry days of previous years, wanted full bowls at every meal.

Mr. Sands had given up writing in his notebooks. He now spent all his time talking about ways of reaching the mainland or scanning the empty horizon for a boat. One afternoon, after he had burst into the house with rain dripping from his oilskins, his hair blown in every direction, and a wild look in his eyes, Catriona found herself thinking about the woman in Grannie's story—the one who had gone crazy from wanting to leave the island.

"Why don't you put a letter in the sea asking them to send a boat like Lady Grange did?" Catriona suggested, watching the visitor shed his coat and take up his usual place in front of the window.

"What do you mean, Catriona?"

He didn't even bother to turn around.

"Lady Grange sent messages to the mainland tied to bits of wood, and a boat finally came and fetched her away."

Mr. Sands was listening now, though he was caught between his interest in a new story about the island and his eagerness to get away from it. Getting away from the island won, but while he whittled a piece of wood into the rough shape of a boat, he kept asking Catriona questions about Lady Grange, until she had nothing left to tell. He sealed a message inside his little boat and burned the words OPEN THIS on the deck with a hot iron rod. One of the sailors came over and added ballast so that the boat would ride level on the water, and Catriona's father added an inflated sheep's bladder to make it float higher. Then Ma let them have a scrap of red cloth for a flag to make the boat more noticeable when it washed up on some mainland beach.

"The St. Kilda mailboat!" Mr. Sands exclaimed, holding it up for everyone to see. "I wager Lady Grange's boat wasn't such a fine ship as this."

"Aye, you'd want a speedier boat than hers," Catriona agreed. " 'Twas seven years before she got an answer!"

When the sailors heard that, they made a second boat from a life buoy with the name *Peti Dubrovacki* on it that had washed up on the beach after the wreck. They tied a bottle to the buoy, with a letter inside it addressed to the Austrian Consul in Glasgow.

The visitor and the sailors, and the islanders too, all waited anxiously for a steady northwest wind. Finally, after much discussion, they decided that the wind was right.

"Can I go and watch, Ma?" Catriona asked when she saw the men setting off for the beach.

"Run along, lass," her mother answered. She was feeling quite cheered by the thought that the sailors might be gone before the summer steamers came, though she was careful not to say so aloud.

They launched the boats on a falling tide with the wind blowing offshore so that they wouldn't just wash back into Village Bay. Catriona followed the men, picking her way carefully over the slippery sea wrack, even though she knew Ma wouldn't have liked her going so far out on the rocks.

Mr. Sands threw his boat in first. A great cheer went up when it bobbed over the first wave and set off across the water with a purposeful look. Then the captain hurled the life buoy–boat into the sea and a wave washed over it. Watching it spin dizzily down the next wave, Catriona felt her whole world begin to spin. She seemed to be one with the spinning boat, no longer on the shore. When another wave lifted the boat, Catriona felt her stomach rise. Cold water sloshed around her and the sound of the sea thundered inside her head. The wind was driving the boat so close against the shore that Catriona could see rivulets of water from the last wave running back down the barnacle-encrusted rock. People were running frantically along the cliff top and someone was moving crablike down its face, but there was surely no way the person could get to her in time.

"Help! Save me!" Catriona screamed.

She reached up and an outstretched hand grabbed hers just as the water swamped the boat, roaring in her ears and knocking the breath clear out of her body.

The girl on the crub stirred and moaned and plucked at the blanket, trying to escape. She had been in and out of sleep—in and out of life—for upward of three days. The shadow of the old woman leaning over to tuck the sheepskin robe back around the sleeping girl took on the humped silhouette of a cormorant feeding its young. She kissed the girl gently, her lips cool against the fevered cheek, then shuffled over to stir the pot simmering on the fire.

The girl opened her eyes, but she could see nothing in the dim room to anchor her to any time at all.

Sometimes when she wakened she felt wee Fiona's warm body cuddled beside her in the box bed; sometimes she could hear the whispering of the crazy woman as she wrote her letters on the margins of pages torn from the black book; and sometimes it was the Old One who spoke in a gentle, coaxing voice, calling her spirit back. She was too tired to bring her own spirit back. That would have to be a struggle between the Old One and the time beyond. And all the while, the girl went in and out of sleep, in and out of life.

"Cathan! Cathan!"

Erik's voice, calling her to the time beyond, drowned out the other voices. She was again standing on the heights of Conochair, and when she turned around there he was, tall and golden, walking toward her, love shining in his eyes.

"Come, Cathan! Come, lass!" he said softly. "Come back down with me to the Beltane fire. Our wedding dance is about to begin."

And then she heard her own voice, shrill and urgent.

"Baine! Baine!"

She was lost in a fog, not knowing which way to go.

"Catie! Where are you, Catie?"

She ran toward the answering shout. The ground gave way beneath her feet, and she went spiraling down into nothingness as she fell.

"Caitlin!"

Fighting her way back from the void, she opened her eyes and saw Dougal's face, dark and frowning, hovering over her. A slow smile changed his features when he saw that she was awake.

"Dougal!"

As she whispered his name she remembered the figure moving crablike across the sheer rock, risking the sea. Then came the memory of an outstretched hand. It had been Dougal who had pulled her from the waves.

"Are you better, lass?" Dougal asked anxiously.

"Aye! And hungry," Caitlin whispered, raising herself on one elbow.

Dougal fetched a pan from the fire and sat by the crub, spooning thin porridge into Caitlin as if she were a babe again. Her hunger was quickly satisfied.

"Where's the Old One?" she asked, looking around the dim room. "She was here, wasn't she?"

"She went to my mother's house to get some sleep—her first rest in three days. Sine and the children have been there since you and Brendan came."

"Brendan!" Caitlin exclaimed. "What can you know about him?"

"Don't you remember Brendan, the stranger who brought you back from Boreray?" Dougal asked. "Everyone was terrified when you and the stranger appeared out of the storm! Even the druids thought he had brought you back from the afterworld and were afraid!"

"Brendan!" Caitlin repeated. "How strange that I should be here and find myself in Brendan's time as well!"

23

BRENDAN

AFTER DOUGAL HAD spotted the boat from the Gap, news of its coming spread quickly from one house to the next across the village. No one had visited them from the outside world in living memory and the islanders were more afraid than curious. They weren't reassured when the druids, who had come over from Gleann Mor to witness the event, stayed well back on the shore, as if they were afraid too. But when the boat finally came into view around the headland of Oiseval and went skimming across the bay toward Dun Gap, it looked so frail and so completely lacking in direction that most people's first thought was to save it. Dougal, followed by a few other men, braved the fierce waves down in Dun Gap, while the rest of the villagers watched from the cliff top.

Fear returned, redoubled, when the men down on the rocks saw the passenger in the boat. The spirit of

Caitlin returning from the sea—or from the after-world! The oarsman had a strange hairless face that bore a marked likeness to a seal. Seal-folk were well known for their dealings with the other world. Even Dougal, who had the advantage of knowing that Caitlin had neither drowned nor fallen from the cliffs when she had disappeared from Hirta nearly two moons before, didn't doubt that he was seeing her spirit. She was so thin that her wet clothes were molded to her bones, and her staring eyes were like black holes in her dead-white face. All the same, when she screamed at him to save her, he dragged her from the water without hesitating and carried her in his arms all the way back to the Old One's house.

The Old One was quick to dispel talk of spirits and seal-folk. The girl was alive—though it might be a struggle to keep her that way. The old woman busied herself with practical worries like building up a hot fire and heating water.

"Get me the warmest skins from your storage cleit," she told Dougal. "Ask Rona if she can spare some dried lousewort and eyebright. Aye, and I'll need water from the Well of Virtues. It has stronger curing powers than the Tobar Well."

"Even though I knew she was on Boreray all this time, I was afraid I was just bringing you her spirit," Dougal confessed.

"So that's where she has been hidden," the Old One

said. "I always suspected you had some knowledge of where she was. But go and fetch everything quickly. We haven't won her back yet."

The men down on the rocks hadn't wanted to see the boat smashed to bits. While they were saving it, they pulled the stranger ashore. He used up more words thanking them than most of them spoke in an entire day. In the face of such gratitude, no one knew what to do, and so they welcomed him, warily, to the village and offered him a vacant house on Ruaival for shelter.

The next morning they brought him small offerings of food, which he ate voraciously, but only after saying a spell over them. Druag, who hadn't snared any fulmar that summer, brought an oatmeal bannock. He was disappointed when, instead of eating it, the stranger broke it into bits and gave a piece to everyone who was there. Though the bannock did get more magic words said over it than all the rest of the food combined.

The days that followed the arrival of the stranger were unseasonably mild, almost as if his coming had cast a spell over the island. Everyone spent hours up on Ruaival listening to him speak. It was hard to fathom the power of the man—for he was not tall and imposing like a druid. He looked undernourished and his cheeks had an unhealthy pallor. His eyes glittered as if he had a fever, and sometimes his stories were interrupted by a dry cough. But the magic of his words made them forget the man. He talked endlessly, telling them about the Maker, who ruled everyone, even the spirits of the afterworld. His God was the only God, the true God, and he claimed that his message was stronger than druid magic.

They learned to call him Brendan. When they asked him where he had found Caitlin, he told them that he had come not just to save her, but to save them all from the fear of the spirits of the afterworld. He often spoke of the Green Island, where he used to live. A land so big that there was no hill where you could stand and see the ocean on the east side and on the west. Although there was enough room on the Green Island for the druids and the followers of Brendan's religion each to have their own place, there had been conflict nonetheless. But they now lived in peace. The monks and priests of the new church performed the ceremonies, and the druids were the keepers of the ballads and songs. When the islanders asked how such a thing had been brought about, Brendan said that the answer was in his black book.

The book lay open on a flat stone inside Brendan's house. Most of the islanders had already seen it, but now that it held so much promise, they crowded close and peered at the strange black marks that could turn into words and stories in Brendan's mind. They pointed to the delicate pictures around the edges of things that had no names. But when Brendan read the words aloud, they were disappointed. *There is no fear in love, but perfect love casts out fear.* It would take a more powerful spell than that to bring peace between them and the druids.

The druids, who had ways of knowing everything that was taking place in the village, were aware that the islanders had rallied around Brendan, and so they made their own presence more noticeable on the island. As the feast day of Samain drew closer, they were suddenly everywhere, hovering near the well on Ruaival or flitting across the moor up on Mullach Sgar like great white moths at dusk. And during the long nights, they invaded the islanders' dreams with warnings that the dark magic was going to usher in the day of the Samain feast. Neil Mor, who was not given to visions, wakened one night, trembling. He broke down and sobbed as he told his terrified wife that he had seen blood dripping from a stone. Others whispered that they had shared the same dream. Word that the Stallir was about to loose the dark magic was on everyone's lips.

When Dougal heard the rumors, he went to see the Old One. Caitlin was asleep on the crub, her red-gold hair spread over her thin shoulders. The Old One had been brushing it before the girl fell asleep.

Dougal didn't know how to begin, but it turned out that he didn't need to tell the Old One what he feared. She already knew that Caitlin had walked with the druids and that her shadow had darkened the stone.

The old woman had learned about it from Caitlin's ravings while the girl had wandered in and out of herself during the worst days of her sickness.

Caitlin stirred in her sleep, and Dougal glanced over at her. She looked stronger now than she had earlier when she had been so surprised to learn that the stranger's name was Brendan.

"She should have stayed on Boreray," the Old One said. "Aye, it might have been better had you not pulled her from the sea. Or had I not called her back from those other places she has been wandering. That might have been the greatest kindness. She was happy in those other places and didn't really want to come back."

"There must be something we can do," Dougal said.

"What about this Brendan everyone's talking about? Could he help her? I haven't had time to hear him myself, but even Druag speaks well of him. Though I don't for the life of me see how Brendan can change what Caitlin herself has set in motion."

"I could ask him to come and see her," Dougal offered. "But he's such a small and hairless man! And not even strong."

When Dougal went up Ruaival to speak to Brendan, he found him, for once, alone. He looked very much as he did the first time Dougal had seen him, but today his face was not dripping with salt spray but glistening with sweat from the effort of prying a stone out of the earth on the hillside.

"Help me move this rock, lad," he said. "I've been struggling with it for hours!"

Together they moved the rock and positioned it close to a wall of stone that Brendan was building.

"What's it going to be?" Dougal asked.

"I'm making a house for the glory of God. I thought when I first saw this island that I could live out the rest of my days in peace, contemplating the ways of God, and leave the cares of his world to someone else, but that is not what He has in mind for me, it seems."

"You'll never keep out the wind with a wall of rocks," Dougal said. "For a house to be warm, you have to dig it into the earth."

"If we make the walls double and pack gravel and earth in between, the house will be drier and warmer than any built underground, and a lot more comfortable." After they had moved another rock, Brendan added, "On the Green Island, we built houses this way that were taller than a man."

"What holds up the roof?"

"We used beams of oak, but here we can use the whale bones on the beach for rafters. Let me show you how it can be done in case I am not here long enough to finish the building myself."

"Where are you going?" Dougal asked.

Brendan didn't answer.

Dougal watched the old man's clever fingers assemble a tiny building from stones and twigs and bird bones. He began to see how a building could be made to stand above the ground, but one man could not do it alone. He said as much to Brendan.

"Aye, that is the beauty of it," the old man answered, smiling. "It will be stronger because people worked together to make it. It will be even stronger if the druids work with your people as well."

"That can never be," Dougal said. "Haven't you heard that the Stallir plans to loose the dark magic on the island on Samain morning? I am afraid that Caitlin . . . the girl you brought back from Boreray . . . is going to die."

"How long do we have till Samain?" Brendan asked. "I've lost all track of time since I came here."

"Three days," Dougal answered.

"Then we must get busy," Brendan answered. "I'm going to need a lot of help if I'm to finish this building in three days."

"How can that save Caitlin?"

"The Maker will show us the way."

All the villagers worked hard, carrying stones and building walls and packing earth down in between. As the walls grew higher they began to see some merit to this new way of building. While they worked, they listened to Brendan's stories. He told them how the Maker had made the light and the dark, the land and the sea, the sun and the moon, the fish and the birds, and finally man and woman. The next story was harder to understand. God grew angry with the world and sent down rain for forty days and forty nights and flooded the land. It often rained on Hirta for forty days and forty nights, but the sea never came anywhere near the top of Conochair. And the birds were able to fly and swim anyway.

As time ran out, Dougal grew dispirited. He couldn't understand why Brendan was putting so much effort into a useless building. How were walls— without even a roof or a door—going to make any difference against the Stallir at Samain? It seemed that Brendan had only talked them into wasting the little time that was left. Aye, talking was all Brendan was good at, Dougal thought bitterly.

Brendan appeared to be dispirited, too, on that last afternoon before Samain. He spent a long time on his knees doing nothing. Then he set off down Ruaival toward the village, walking slowly, as if each step pained him.

Caitlin was awake when Brendan came to the house, and she was glad to see him. Her strength had returned these last few days, and some of her former impatience with it. She didn't like the way the Old One was keeping her out of everyone's way.

"Do you know what day this is?" Brendan asked, once their greetings were over.

Caitlin shook her head.

"It is the eve of the Samain feast."

"Hush!" the Old One said. She'd been watching

Brendan suspiciously from the moment he'd come into the house, and now she looked as if she were going to drive him away. "The child has enough to worry about without hearing that!"

"I want you to come up to my house on Ruaival tonight," Brendan said, taking Caitlin's thin hand in his. "If the Stallir or one of the druids come, I would not want them to find you here. I had hoped the house we are building on Ruaival would be finished, but that is of no account. The Maker has his own way of protecting his children. Will you come?"

Caitlin nodded. There were a great many questions she would have liked to ask Brendan, but he looked so drawn and tired that she didn't want to bother him. Just before he got up to go, he told Caitlin there would be peace on the island only when they learned to love one another, because perfect love casts out fear.

"And when you have made the first beginnings of peace, look forward and not back," he warned her. "Dream of the children that are waiting to be born, and don't weep for the scars of the old people. Bear in mind that the hopes of Hirta lie in its future, not the lingering pains of its past."

After he had gone, Caitlin lay in the crub thinking about the future she had seen. Lady Grange and blind Baine; Donald Mac Ghillie in Cathan's time; and Catriona's old grandfather, who had given the half-drowned sailor his best suit. Running through all of it had been a thread of love—not perfect love, by any means, for sometimes it had been stretched thinner than a sinew snare. Yet it had been strong enough to bind one time to the next.

But for the life of her, she still could not see how this frail man could save the island from the dark side of the Stallir's magic.

24

ᚦHE SACRIFICE

As CAITLIN MADE her way up Ruaival in the gathering
dusk her thoughts were with the Old One, who had
followed her to the cottage door, not wanting her to go
out. "The dark magic is abroad tonight," she had said,
her voice quavering. "I feel it in my bones."

Caitlin had hugged her, surprising them both. The
old woman had felt as brittle and frail as a fledgling
bird in her arms.

The walls of Brendan's building stood directly
ahead, taller than they had been that day when
Grannie MacCrimmon rested there instead of going to
church. It was reassuring to see this link with the
future rising in her own time. But moments later
Caitlin was jerked back to the awful uncertainties of
the present. A white-clad figure stepped out from
behind the rising walls and headed toward Brendan's
underground house. He went in without any hesita-
tion, as if someone were expecting him. What business

could any of the druids have with Brendan? Unless the dark side had already won.

Remembering the Old One's foreboding, Caitlin turned and ran back down the hill, angling toward the bay to put as much distance as she could between the druid and herself. She had no intention of going near Brendan if he was having dealings with the druids. She had reached the big boulder—the one she used to climb when she was small—when she saw a tall figure blocking her way. The Stallir! Looking up into his winter eyes, Caitlin was too frightened to move, too frightened to cry out. Perhaps the dark magic held her still.

She had no clear memory of what happened next. Just that she was suddenly alone in one of the old cleits high on Conochair, her wrists bound behind her back, her ankles tied. She had walked a while, she thought, until her legs had folded under her. And then the druid had carried her, limp as a dead gannet. It had taken no time at all to climb the heights of Conochair. Now, knowing what morning would bring, she wanted to make every second last. If she could only escape to the time beyond . . . but there was nowhere to go. . . . And tomorrow morning the sacrifice stone would be red with blood.

She mustn't think about that . . .

Instead, she thought herself back to climbing with Tormod Rudh. She remembered the day she had struggled up the rock face of Dun and how far above her Tormod Rudh had seemed. She'd thought she'd never reach the top, but worse than falling would have been admitting that she was afraid! Even when the cliff above her had appeared as smooth as a gannet's egg, her groping fingers had found a crack. Then Tormod had reached down and pulled her up to the top. For a moment she'd thought he was angry and she'd wished herself back at the bottom, but then his pride in her courage had shown through, and they'd both laughed.

Caitlin smiled in the darkness. Moments later her stomach lurched as if a foothold had crumbled on the cliff. Someone was moving the big rock that served as a door. Surely the night could not have flown so soon. Now someone was inside the cleit with her. She could hear the person breathing, but it was so dark she couldn't even tell if it was a white-cloaked druid.

"Caitlin! Where are you, child? Are you awake?"

The voice was low and musical.

Feadair!

Caitlin flattened herself against the stones behind her. Her thumping heart was giving her away. He was moving stealthily closer.

"Caitlin, lass! Where are you? We must be quick, for I don't know how long the guard will sleep."

A feather of hope stirred.

"I'm over here," Caitlin whispered. "My legs and wrists are tied. I can't move."

She felt Feadair's long fingers fumbling with the

knots. His breath was soft against her hair. Had he really come to save her? She couldn't let herself believe it, even when he gently rubbed her wrists to take away the pain of the rope, even when he led her past the sleeping guard.

She'd never seen the stars shine so brightly and the freshness of the air made her head spin. She didn't really care now where Feadair took her so long as she could feel the wind.

But he had stopped in front of a narrow slit in the hillside.

"No!" Caitlin shouted, trying to push him away.

Her protest was cut short by a hand pressed against her mouth.

"You have to hide again, Caitlin," Feadair whispered urgently. "You must stay out of sight until after the sun has risen tomorrow. You'll be safe here. Trust me! If you promise to stay hidden, this time there'll be no ropes or guards."

Feadair pushed her through the opening. It was so narrow that he couldn't follow her, and by the time she'd eased herself around in the tiny crevice and pulled her cloak close about her shoulders, he was gone. She wished she'd asked him to tell her what was going to happen. She sniffed the dank earth. She'd exchanged a puffin's snare for a puffin's burrow . . . but that was better than a grave. She closed her eyes and must have slept because she was suddenly jerked back to wakefulness, shivering all over.

The Sacrifice

Something terrible was going to happen.

She wriggled out of the crevice, leaving her wool cloak behind. The morning air was damp, and now she shivered from the cold in her skimpy wool shift. Overhead the stars were fading and the eastern sky was turning red and gold, lit by the first rays of the rising sun.

A scream—hollow, echoing, anguished—pierced the dawn. Weaving and stumbling, Caitlin began to run toward the sound. The druids were standing in a circle around the stones and in their midst stood the Stallir, a knife in his upraised hand. His white robe was spattered scarlet with drops of blood. Then Caitlin saw, either in reality or in her mind—looking back, she was never sure—a white-robed, hooded figure slumped over the sacrifice stone, which was running with blood. The druids began to sing, their voices echoing the haunting cries of birds on a summer night. They fell into place behind the Stallir, who had lifted up the sacrifice in his arms, the face and head hidden by the hood, which was dazzling white in contrast to the blood-soaked folds that covered the body. He led the procession toward the place where Conochair dropped straight down to the sea.

Caitlin followed them to the cliff's edge and saw the Stallir release the body. It floated slowly down—as light as a bird with all the blood drained out of it. The wind pulled away the white hood covering the face and head. Surely it wasn't . . . it couldn't be . . .

Caitlin screamed in horror.

Brendan, the stranger, had been sacrificed in her place. How could such a thing have happened? She screamed again, and before her screams died away the druids had turned back from the cliff and were all staring at her, the horror and fear in their eyes no less than in her own. The Stallir, his face white and stretched, his eyes wide, was still on the edge of the cliff. He took a step away from her and lost his footing. For a long moment the only sound on the whole island was the rattling of a few stones dribbling over the lip of Conochair where the Stallir had disappeared. Feadair had reached out to save him, but was too late.

Feadair didn't look over the edge. Instead he walked slowly back toward Caitlin.

"I told you to stay hidden!"

"I would have shown myself sooner if I'd known that Brendan was going to be killed," Caitlin answered.

"Brendan insisted this was the way it had to be," Feadair explained softly. "He didn't have long to live anyway. By his death, he said, the dark side of the magic could be defeated and peace would come to the island."

"But he was a good man . . ."

Gently Feadair led Caitlin back toward the stones. The druids followed and encircled them as if they were taking part in some long-rehearsed ceremony. At first Caitlin thought that their stunned faces reflected her own horror and guilt at the way Brendan had died, but Feadair seemed to be saying that, even now, they still thought they had witnessed Caitlin's death.

"Brendan's face was covered," Feadair said. "No one else knows that he took your place inside the cleit. It was your blood they saw spilled on the stone and your body they saw the Stallir throw over Conochair. And now they think that you have returned from the afterworld."

As they waited for her to speak, even their druid cloaks couldn't conceal their shaking knees and pounding hearts. Horror still stared from their eyes. They had just seen the spirits claim their chief and send a young girl back from the afterworld in his place. The balance of fear had shifted, so Caitlin could do anything now. But she knew that Brendan hadn't given his life to replace an old fear with a new one. He had told her that there is no fear in love. Had he faced death without fear, she wondered.

She looked at the druids defiantly, the wind blowing through her long red hair.

"That was Brendan, the stranger, whom you saw die," she shouted. "It wasn't me. I bring you no message from the afterworld! My message is from the time that is yet to come. We must do away with the fear that has divided us. Tonight, let us take the first step together when you meet with the islanders for the Feast of Samain."

Nobody moved. It was hard to tell what they

thought or what they were going to do. And Caitlin wasn't sure how the villagers would respond later when she told them that Brendan had faced the Stallir's dark magic for Hirta's sake, believing that love was stronger than fear. But she did know what Feadair thought. He was looking down at her with the same pride that she had seen in Tormod Rudh's face after she had climbed the rocks of Dun all by herself. She smiled shyly up at him. And he smiled back.

25

THE SAMAIN FEAST

THE LIGHT WAS so poor that Caitlin didn't see the first
group of villagers coming out of the houses nearest the
shore. Even when they were almost level with the
dyke where she'd been waiting, she couldn't tell how
much they were carrying because they had their wool
cloaks pulled close about them. They had been joined
by men and women and children from nearly every
house in the village. Caitlin had known she could
count on Dougal and the Old One. And on Barra and
Sine and their children. Perhaps on Neil Mor. She
hadn't been sure how many more would come. And
she still didn't know if they'd agreed about the gifts.

After she'd come back from Conochair that morning, she had gone to every house and had told them
about the Stallir calling down the dark magic and how
Brendan's blood had stained the sacrifice stone. Gareth
had responded for most people when he said that the
Stallir had been defeated by his own dark magic, so

the time was surely right for them to drive out the druids.

"No! Our real enemy is our fear of the Spirits of Darkness," Caitlin told Gareth. "Defeating the druids won't do away with that. Brendan said that only love can cast out fear."

At least Gareth had relented and joined those villagers who were now making their way to the Place of the Dead. He was walking with the Old One. Caitlin fell into step beside them.

When they had all reached the great mound of driftwood and heather and bracken that had been gathered weeks ago for the fire, they waited for the druids to come, as they had so many times before. Their dark eyes were fixed on the top of the pass.

"There they are!" one of Sine's little ones sang out.

"Hush!" Sine said.

Her attention was diverted from the three columns of white-clad druids flowing down the hillside when her youngest child dropped his basket in the mud. She scooped up the bird meat and scolded him.

"The Stallir's place is empty!" someone whispered.

"The seer is carrying the sacred flame."

The islanders watched the druids split into two groups and form a half circle in front of them. An awkward silence fell, almost as if no one knew what was supposed to happen next. Then Sine's children surged forward with their gifts. Other little ones, equally excited at having baskets to carry this year, pushed in after them, giggling. Their parents followed. Dougal handed Caitlin a basket and she joined the rest. They had listened to her after all. All the baskets were more or less the same, with the bird meat carefully divided among them. They would not have to fear the anger of the spirit world because no one had given less than another. It was only one small step, but they were taking it together.

When the seer called the spirits back, the villagers burst into a spontaneous cheer. Even after what they'd given to the druids, no one would go hungry this winter if they shared what they had left. Then the seer thrust the torch into the heart of the fire. Although it wasn't raining, the fire seemed to take a long time to catch hold. The villagers cheered again when the flame sputtered along a branch. They were looking forward to the roast mutton.

Feadair, who was standing close to Caitlin, tuned up his harp. As he began to sing, everyone—druids and villagers—drew closer to hear the words. His song was about the bravery of the hunters who soared across the face of Conochair like birds without wings. Then he sang about the most fearless hunter of them all, a hero who would live forever. A hero called Tormod Rudh.

Feadair's song was the second small step.

Dougal reached out and took Caitlin's hand. And that was the third small step. Caitlin smiled at Dougal, remembering Brendan's words. The hope for Hirta lay in the future and not in the pains of the past.

MARGARET J. ANDERSON

was born in Scotland and graduated from the University of Edinburgh with a degree in genetics. A writer with a special talent for evoking the past, Anderson for many years has been fascinated with the intriguing history and rugged beauty of Scotland's St. Kilda Islands. And it was against the spectacular backdrop of these now abandoned islands that she first began the adventure that was to become *The Druid's Gift*. But it was only when she actually visited the islands on an archaeological dig in 1988, and herself stood among the low stone houses of the medieval village huddled together against the howling winds, that fact met fantasy and the ancient drama of the islands' buried past fully emerged.

Margaret J. Anderson is the author of many books, including *The Mists of Time, The Journey of the Shadow Bairns, Searching for Shona*, and *In the Keep of Time*. She lives in Corvallis, Oregon, with her professor husband. They have four children.